C000225389

# SOR

Daniel Bird

**Signal 8 Press**
**Truro, Cornwall**
**United Kingdom**

'What a piece of work is a man! how noble in reason! how infinite in faculty! in form and moving how express and admirable! in action how like an angel! in apprehension how like a god!'

- William Shakespeare, *Hamlet*

'I left the room with silent dignity, but caught my foot in the mat.'

- George and Weedon Grossmith, *Diary of a Nobody*

## Praise for *Sorry Men* by Daniel Bird

"*Sorry Men* is a knowing and absurdist lark—a jolt of flash fiction that comes out jabbing and keeps jabbing as the sorry men found therein are not only sorry, but lacking—not nearly as smart as they might be, yet etched with honesty and empathy by Bird, an artist in miniature, and loving portraitist of the delusional."

- Ben Tanzer, author of *The Missing, Upstate, Be Cool,* and *Orphans*

"This compendium of words is like the Netflix series *Black Mirror* in that you don't quite know what any given story is going for but you are happy they are short and happy that there are enough of them that you can bail out on any one, comfortable in the knowledge that there's plenty left if you can't sleep or get *Black Mirror* on Netflix."

- Doug Stanhope, comedian

"Daniel Bird's brief, but vivid, stories hit me like a literary Instagram feed, catapulting me to so many places so quickly, I needed a seat belt to stay anchored to my chair. Some stories disturbed me like a good Neil LaBute play, others left me gasping at the finish line at their O. Henry plot twist. What's best, in Bird's 'Sorry' world there's a story for everyone: some are tender, some are humorous, and some just a wee bit dangerous."

- Charlie Schroeder, author, *Man of War*

"Bird's sharp-witted satire quietly introduces us to a host of characters doing their best (or, quite frankly, not at times) to navigate a modern world that seems confusingly at odds to their hardwiring. This collection of short stories paints a hilarious portrait of modern society with moments of laugh-out-loud humour, savage irony, and 'head in hands' frustration."

- Anna Passey, actress

"Frustrating, farcical, futile, and very funny."

- Jason Wong, actor

"A collection of funny little razorblades."

- Jason Tobin, actor

"With *Sorry Men*, Bird has given us a collection of literary diamonds that masterfully explore the challenges of seeking human connection in the modern world. Highly recommended!"

- G. Riley Mills, Emmy Award-winning writer, *The Lost Story of Emmett Till: Trial in the Delta*

**Sorry Men**

By Daniel Bird

Published by Signal 8 Press

An imprint of Signal 8 Press Limited

Copyright 2024 Daniel Bird

ISBN (print): 978-1-915531-06-3

eISBN: 978-1-915531-07-0

Daniel Bird has asserted his right under the Copyright, Designs and Patents Act, 1988, to be identified as the author of this work.

Cover design: Cristian Checcanin

Author photo: Frankie Adamson

Signal 8 Press Limited

Truro, Cornwall

United Kingdom

Website: www.signal8press.com

*In gratitude to my grandparents.*

*For their love, laughter, wisdom, and tireless
support of my endeavours.
And, without whom,
I would truly be a sorry man.*

# TABLE OF CONTENTS

# JAR

ABBIE hadn't put it on the list of her things she wanted back. And it seemed far too nice to throw away. She used to fill that glass jar with the heart-shaped cookies she baked for me at weekends.

One Saturday night, I soaked it in hot, soapy water, removing the last of the crumbs, and started using it for loose change. I planned to treat myself to something really special when the jar was full. It would be my special reward for getting over Abbie. Every now and then, I'd pause before turning off the lamp just to marvel at the jar on my bedside table. It was filling up. A testament to my patience and self-control. Each new layer of coins showed how little I was thinking about her.

It took a year, but finally the jar was full. I took it to the bank, planning on a little shopping spree for the new me. When I proudly presented my jar to the teller, I noticed he looked a little tired. Through the perforated holes in the thick plastic screen between us, he exhaled and asked why I was doing this and why I wasn't instead using one of the many machines available at the nearby supermarket. I showed him my creased photo of Abbie I kept in my wallet and explained I'd like to open a separate account for this fund. He didn't comment on her pretty face. In fact, his expression betrayed a hint of impatience. After turning to roll his eyes at a colleague—who was in fits of laughter about something—the teller gestured for me to pour my coins into the little tray at the bottom of his screen. The lid on the jar was stuck and I had great difficulty getting the thing open. A man in the queue behind me exhaled loudly. Someone else clicked their tongue. After approximately two minutes, a very helpful person—

hidden from view near the back of the queue—suggested smashing the jar to save everyone's time, for crying out loud. I felt this was good advice. And, after an unproductive pause, my eyes fell on the velvet rope shepherding the dozen or so people behind me into an orderly queue. The base of the metal stanchion holding the rope looked strong enough. It worked on the third try. Some coins rolled under the desk of a suited man promoting loans to small businesses. Others scurried across the floor and under the manager's fish tank. I watched as a number of waiting customers dropped my coins into the charitable donation boxes around the bank's lobby; others pocketed the coins for themselves. The amount I eventually managed to retrieve was only enough for a bus fare across town. The teller told me as much while his colleague dabbed away tears with his tie.

On my walk home, I passed a fancy new shop that sold kitchenware and scented candles. I was peering closely at the display, a shop assistant with a spotless apron smiled at me. The display was almost as beautiful as she was, but I hadn't the courage to tell her. Instead, in a moment of the very spontaneity Abbie had complained was so uncharacteristic of me, I spent the remaining money I'd saved (and a fair bit more) on a new jar. I didn't explain where the money had come from. However, I did ask the assistant to help me test whether I'd be able to open the jar after I'd forced it closed with two of the hefty gluten-free recipe cookbooks also on sale in the shop. She was incredibly helpful and, for a brief moment, I confess she reminded me of Abbie. I was trying to explain how this new jar was assuredly the most superior jar I'd ever owned, when my voice caught on an unexpected fragment of emotion. I couldn't finish my remarks, so instead I paid in silence while the assistant smiled at me. A little embarrassment aside, I left the shop knowing I wasn't going to lose anything next time.

# DOG

JIMBO was as lovable and trustworthy as any four-legged best friend to a man. Much to my surprise, he'd also proven incredibly gifted. By his second birthday, he'd mastered over fifty commands and responded to each without hesitation. He never lied. He was house-trained. When we visited hospices during weekends, he would allow withered hands to stroke his obedient skull for hours. He brought me whatever I asked, provided he could fit it in his mouth. At night, he shared my bed. And during the day, he was always at my feet. By his eighth birthday, I was certain he was the cleverest dog in the world.

One day, on a walk beside the river, Jimbo and I saw a father skimming stones with his son. They were having a contest, and the young boy was doing rather well, jumping up and down with delight. The father scoffed and made such a tremendous effort on his next turn that he knocked the boy over with his swinging arm. The boy fell into the water, and the current dragged him swiftly towards the weir. Yelling, his father ran down the bank trying to reach him. Fortunately, I was downstream with Jimbo. I whistled three times and pointed at the struggling child. Jimbo's eyes widened and, in an instant, he was sprinting to the rescue. The boy was metres from plunging into the churning water below the weir when Jimbo leapt into the river. He grabbed the boy and dragged him to the safety of the riverside.

Moments later, the father appeared, bent over breathless, his hands on his muddy knees. "Thank you. Thank you," he panted, his eyes moist. I sensibly suggested how lucky it was that Jimbo had been here. Further to this, I highlighted the importance of taking great care of children near fast-flowing water. My dog had risked his life to save the boy. I was surprised at the tumble of words from my mouth and the fact my voice was much louder than usual. The father stood up straight and pointed out that one of Jimbo's teeth had nicked his son's thumb. In fact, it was bleeding. "Look at what your mutt did to my boy!" he bellowed, pulling the boy protectively behind him.

The next day, a sign printed on A4 paper was stuck to the gate of the field where Jimbo and I often walked. It warned ramblers and other interested people about a 'viscous dog' alongside a watermarked photo of a breed remarkably similar to Jimbo. A few days later, a woman with her daughter in tow crossed the road specifically to avoid Jimbo. I then received a letter that informed me the father was pressing charges. His expensive solicitor, who wore a yellow silk tie, successfully argued that Jimbo was a "dangerous canine" and should be put down.

The following week, I stroked Jimbo's paw and pressed my face into his gradually motionless chest. The veterinary assistant squeezed my shoulder as I sobbed. Through tear-choked words and mouth half full of his hair, I asked if it would ever be possible to train an animal out of its primitive instincts.

# JAILBIRD

**S**AM hung his tattooed arms through the bars, muscular enough to defend himself, but slender enough to enjoy the breeze. He was one of the few imprisoned there who could see the sea and at each inmate review, he'd thank the board for that. The warden would merely nod whilst continuing to make notes. Politeness or good behaviour wouldn't shorten Sam's sentence and he felt increasingly hopeless about how he would get through the remaining time. The sea view was his only respite from his gloomy outlook.

At sunrise, Sam loved to look out over the quay. The past week, he'd had the blessed good fortune to witness a group of mime artists and acrobats rehearsing their work. The tumblers would climb on one another's shoulders up in the salty air before dropping down onto the straw mats they'd laid out in the morning. Sam watched as they gradually improved. Their production was an epic story of sorrow and loss. The protagonist seemed to be a runaway prisoner who found his true love on a ship, before losing her when the vessel docked. Sam was desperate to know whether the lovers would reunite, but the company never reached the final act. The director was prone to interrupt and shout in frustration when the cast made small errors. More than anyone else, he'd yell at the mime who played the runaway prisoner's true love.

As the cast left after one particularly gruelling rehearsal, Sam noticed her sitting on her suitcase, weeping. He yelled to get her attention, but she couldn't hear, so he waved his bed sheet out between the bars. Catching sight of the flailing material, she dried her eyes as Sam gestured as clearly as he could that she was a fantastic actress and that she should not give up. The mime beamed and pretended to pull a heavy rope for a moment before waving goodbye.

For the next few days, Sam kept watching the rehearsals. After each show he and the mime had what simple conversations they could using hand signals and enthusiastic gestures. Sam learned that she was a 25-year-old travelling actress who dreamed of stardom. He also revealed that he'd been rightfully convicted of robbery, but—if he kept up his good behaviour—he'd be released in the next five years.

Sam's cell no longer felt like a prison. It was the front row in a theatre. On the last day of rehearsals his throat ached as he watched the end of their dumbshow. The story culminated with the escaped prisoner and his beloved reunited in a new country where they got married. His new friend's performance was astonishing. Even the director shook her hand. When the last rehearsal ended, she waved Sam goodbye, gesturing that she was off to tour the world with her show. First, Europe, next North Africa, and eventually, New York, where she planned to pursue stardom. Sam's private theatre was gone, but the rehearsals left him inspired. He worked harder in his wood-shop shifts, helped in the canteen, and—after four more years—Sam was granted his freedom.

Taking the money he'd earned doing carpentry, he bought new clothes, enjoyed an ale, and spent the remainder on the cheapest ticket to New York he could find. He didn't know the mime's name, but that was irrelevant. Every feature, each expert movement and gesture glimpsed from afar was locked in his memory. Since she was doubtless performing on a Broadway stage, she wouldn't be hard to find. Sam strolled past tearful farewells, grateful it wasn't him saying goodbye—he now led a life of new beginnings. He handed over his ticket, made his way up the gangway, and found a spot at the railing. As Sam stared out into the distance, he saw his bleak life in jail and prayed that he'd never see it again. With a renewed sense of confidence, Sam felt as 'unsinkable' as the iconic, steel-plated ship he'd just boarded. As the vessel departed, he waved teary farewells to strangers on the dock as if they were his own family.

# TATTOOS

STEVEN'S eyes were moist with pride as he stuck Sophie's latest drawing to the wall. Although, yes, to the *thoughtless passerby*, the picture might very well *seem* like a mess of squiggly lines, handprints, and a series of distorted, nesting squares, but not to Steven. To him, the artistic vision was crystal clear: 'house'.

"I made this beautiful girl and she made this. It's a miracle!" He'd invited his friend round to see the growing collection. Her whole oeuvre comprised of over a hundred pieces, all created since she'd started primary school.

Steven watched as his friend absorbed the unusual room. A potato-print picture of a butterfly peeled off the ceiling and hit the floor; the humidity was curling the edges of the art; and some of the colours had begun to fade. "Are you sure they'll keep like this?" asked his friend. "I mean, it's lovely, mate, really, but why don't you put them in a scrapbook? Or something?" Steven's gaze fell on a nearby photo of his wife. She'd been living elsewhere and seemed to be contemplating divorce. The scrapbook idea was something she'd also mentioned, although less delicately than his friend.

"But, if I do that," Steven explained, with a lump in his throat, "I won't be able to see them all of the time."

Still, it was enough to make him feel alarmed. *What if* the pictures *did* get ruined? His lifelong messiness was on a seemingly insoluble collision course with the urgent need to see his daughter's work whenever he liked. Nonetheless, Steven thought hard and devised what he considered an optimal solution. Steven took down his favourite picture, entitled 'Magical Flying Rainbow Pony Called Tracy', and soon enough, he was beaming down at a precise copy of 'Magical Flying Rainbow Pony Called Tracy' tattooed on his forearm. He could roll up his sleeve whenever he felt like it, and there it was. Gradually, Steven's skin became a gallery of his daughter's efforts. Before long, he was running out of space. Mirrors were needed to see some of the tattoos, but still, he loved to show them off. For example, in the changing rooms, he could show others present simply by spreading a little flesh apart to reveal a happy sun next to a sausage dog.

"There *is* space for one more!" he told his angelic daughter. "This one's going across my chest. I reserved it. Put it in an envelope, my pumpkin and Daddy will give it to the tattooist. I won't even see it—it'll be a wonderful surprise!"

"Daddy, you're very silly," she giggled. And the very next week, she produced a new drawing.

All it took was six hours of agonising needlework, followed by a long, painkiller- and booze-inspired snooze, and it was done. That weekend, slowly and carefully, Steven unwrapped the layers of bandages in front of his daughter. She was delighted by how colourful and special her father looked. Steven looked down, frowning.

"You're such a silly monkey. Daddy doesn't have blonde hair!"

"That's not *you*, Daddy!" His pig-tailed Princess pointed at the stick man and stick woman who now held hands between his hairless nipples in front of a bright yellow sun. "That's Mickey! Mummy's new friend. Mickey who got me my new pink bike!"

Steven peered through the thick glass partition at his wife, whose face was filled with guilt. When she wouldn't meet his eye, fury overtook his thoughts. Steven pounded his meaty, tattooed hands on the partition, setting off the alarm. Thick arms wrapped around Steven, grating over his tender skin. He kicked and screamed, but it was no good: the guards dragged him away easily. Sophie watched her colourful father gradually disappear, his desperate grip on the corner of the wall exhibiting Tracy, her Magical Flying Rainbow Pony, and a juicy carrot on each of his whitening fingers.

# BLESSING

**C**LAIRE said yes. Giddy with the romance of it, we began to make plans immediately. The following week, I bumped into Sarah at Oak House Deli. She was there with a pram, inside of which was a quiet, fat baby who had her eyes. When I told her about my engagement, she dropped her cheese and pulled me into a hug that lasted some time. I left, clutching slices of wafer-thin breaded ham and intending to head home. But somehow, I found myself in the lobby of Maria's office just as she came through the revolving doors after her lunch break. There was a speck of pesto in her teeth, but they were still blazing white after the procedure she'd had in Bangkok last June. When I showed her a photo of Claire wearing the ring, she clasped my hands in hers and smoothed her thumbs over them in small, concentric circles. She was so pleased for me and insisted I must, *absolutely must*, stay in touch.

Elizabeth was an A & E nurse. When I walked into her ward, I was holding the top table napkin samples. She was marching purposefully towards the lift, but when she saw me, she removed her blood-smeared latex gloves and came over. She squeezed my stubbly face as I shared the news. She seemed elated, saying that I deserved to be with someone who clearly loved me so much. We walked out into the fading daylight of the car park where she began assisting a paramedic performing CPR in the back of an ambulance. This took me back to the time Katie had fainted. I'd surprised her with a fake spider while she was retiling the bathroom. Inspired, I hopped onto a train and grabbed a cab to her place. Strolling past a newly installed water feature on the front lawn, I knocked on her door. Nobody answered. After an hour, I gave up. Since it was school holidays, she was most likely away.

It was quite late when I finally got home. Claire was sitting with her arms crossed on the sofa. My dinner was in the kitchen sink; I counted five and a half little potatoes floating in the water. "Is this how it is going to be?" she eventually said, her voice more tearful than any reasonable person might expect. "No call. No note. No clue where you were." I muttered some apologies, explaining I'd got carried away with wedding arrangements. Claire's expression remained sceptical. I also mentioned I had remembered to buy the wafer-thin slices of breaded ham she'd wanted. Claire stood up and met my gaze. A frown crinkled her brow as she rifled through the camping rucksack I'd dropped on the floor. It overflowed with photos of us, wedding venue brochures, bouquet designs, and the Polaroids of her laughing—ones I'd kept beside my bed before she moved in. Finally, she stopped looking through the bag, exhaling slowly. "You know, I was worried when I saw all this had gone. I thought you'd gone and changed your mind or something."

Immediately, I wrapped her up in a hug, reassuring her a thousand times that I, of course, hadn't changed my mind. I'd just wanted to share the good news. Claire's arms dropped to her sides as she said, "I get it, baby, but you took all this stuff. Andrew popped over for a coffee. I'd nothing to show him. It was a bit embarrassing."

I remembered Andrew. He was the guy who hadn't returned her DVDs. "Oh. Andrew. I thought he'd met someone else?"

"What's that got to do with any of it?" said Claire, pulling away from me. "We just had a little catch-up. He gave me a pedicure. That's all."

"A pedicure?" I said, spotting her bright red toenails for the first time.

"Yeah. Since you took all our wedding stuff what else were we supposed to do?" I nodded in agreement and began spreading out the matrimonial paraphernalia on the dining table, exactly as I'd found it that morning. I paused over the honeymoon brochure. Flicking through it, I found myself wondering where Katie might have gone on holiday. After all, she really hated the sea.

# STAR

MY head had been pressing against the oval window for a while and, feeling cold, I moved, leaving behind a small mark on the glass. We were high above London. I'd successfully slept through my least favourite part of the flight. Stretching a little, I bumped into the passenger on my right. That was a shame. I thought I'd get away with having a spare seat for the whole journey. I sat straight and muttered an apology. "It's OK," she said in a gravelly US accent that seemed to leave footprints on my eardrums. I looked up, taking in her hair, which hung loosely around angular cheekbones. I did a double take. It was her: the pretty actress from that film I saw with Peggy last week, the one Peggy had paused halfway through to announce that she thought the lead actress was haughty. Turning to face me, the actress smiled, eyes shielded under the peak of her baseball cap. I saw from her guarded expression—like she'd been caught red-handed stealing something she didn't want—that she was who she was. Obviously, she didn't want a fuss.

Nonetheless, it was impossible to hide the recognition in my eyes, so I didn't bother. "Oh, you're erm... well you know who you are... and you're travelling cattle class?" It was a really stupid thing to say, but it was what came out. I smiled straight after by way of apology. She looked around at the dozen or so people who could, at any minute, turn and see who she was, potentially making this a nightmare experience for her. "My agent, he made a mistake with the booking. It was last minute and, no offence, but I'm usually up front."

I wasn't offended but I was absolutely astounded by how beautiful she was. She seemed larger than the average human being, but not in a grotesque way. Like an Italian statue in a museum, all chiselled but smelling of bath salts. I hadn't met a famous person before and a sudden flurry of emotions left me feeling flummoxed. Placing my hands under the complimentary blanket, I wrenched off my wedding ring, which elicited a sharp pain. "Say," she said, leaning closer, her breath like silk wafting in the air. "Would you mind if we, erm… It's just…" she gestured around her. She wanted to swap seats. I obliged, immediately standing up and clambering over her into the aisle with great enthusiasm and muttering apologies for when my knee touched hers. She slid over to the more private window seat while I casually stretched my legs and scratched the tip of my nose to convey absolute confidence.

After pumping my chest muscles a bit and tapping a jaunty rhythm on the overhead locker, I sat down with a bump; my wedding ring leapt out of my shirt pocket, onto the floor. "You dropped something there, Mr Kind Stranger," she said playfully. She picked up the gold band, turning it in her fingers for a few moments before glancing at my hand. The strip of pale and slightly bloody skin around where the ring had sat for 18 years stood out vividly. She cocked her head and held my gaze, allowing a long, confident silence. "I do that sometimes too," she said, tossing the band into my lap and patting my groin like an obedient bullmastiff. After she'd turned to the window and closed her eyes, seemingly acting her way to sleep, I was left staring at my tray table and the top of the safety information. After a few minutes of silence, I forced the ring back on. Then the drinks trolley bashed into my knee.

# LOOKING

"**I**T'S definitely somewhere around here," she said, leaning into the road to get a better view down to the end of the street.

"Are you sure?" I said, trying to conceal the extent of my doubt that she knew where she was going. She replied as if she hadn't heard me.

"Maggie said it was near the gym, and the gym is just here, so."

"Which gym?" I inquired as if I hadn't already asked. She didn't know. A plane passed overhead, its sound yet to reach our ears. Angling for a sympathetic yet quizzical tone, I asked if she was *certain* it would be open. She responded that she "would have thought so," her tone seeming to imply the very idea it might be closed was straight out of an asylum.

"No reason it should be closed on a Sunday," she added, with the same edge to her voice that I'd noticed when we were searching for the shop yesterday. I checked my watch, feeling a tiny bubble of worry that we may not be able to get back to the hotel, pack, check out, and reach the airport in 46 minutes.

"Oh, oh, oh! Hold it more this way," she said as if I were a naughty child. I adjusted my grip on the umbrella so she wouldn't get wet. A car whizzed past, beeping its horn.

"Watch out, babe!" I said, trying to defuse my gut-wrenching dread. I let out a little chuckle.

"Oh, do you mind, honey?" she said with a very authentic hint of inquiry, squeezing my cheeks in her hands as if I were a prize-winning Shar Pei.

"I've wasted *your* whole day looking for this place." The emphasis she placed on 'your' immediately triggered a sense of regret for my own selfishness.

"Of course, I don't mind, babe," I said. To support this notion, I assured her that I'd happily spend all week looking for this place with her, if that's what she wanted. In fact, I was halfway to achieving that already.

"I know you would, honey," she said, leaning out into screeching, dirty traffic.

As she looked up at all the street signs in wonder, I stared at her beautiful neck. Our first holiday together and it couldn't be more perfect.

# STEPS

TIM squeezed his way onto the escalator as best he could in the cavernous station. It was jam-packed. His tie was badly knotted and his eyes were bleary. But when a voice he knew called out his name, the stress of rush hour melted away. Nicole was ascending on the other side. She waved at him eagerly. He hadn't seen Nicole for almost a year, but he knew her well enough to infer—from the way her hair curled slightly upward at the tips—that she'd also woken up late. He recalled the times he had observed her straightening it on their bed, oblivious to the persistent wail of the kettle or the fact he might trip on the wire again.

"TimTim!" Nicole called out. Several commuters turned to look. This wouldn't have bothered Nicole, but Tim could feel his face flush.

"Oh hi!" he replied at a much lower volume as they started to draw level.

"How *are* you? Look at your tie!" she laughed as they drew level.

"Oh, great thanks, yeah. And you?" he muttered, glancing around.

"I'm okay!" she chirped, slowly passing him on her continual ascent. She pulled a glum face which he had to turn around to see. "But listen! I had to have Terence put down!" she called out.

Tim raised his voice: "You had Terence, what? What happened? Wait. Let's…" Nicole gestured that she could no longer hear him.

He arrived at the bottom of the escalator and looked up. It stretched on for too long to see all the way to its summit.

He paused for a moment, pondering whether to hop onto the upward escalator or wait for Nicole to come to him. Deciding it would be more chivalrous to go after her, he hopped onto the ascending escalator on which he'd just seen her. About halfway up he saw Nicole stepping onto the downward escalator. It was too late to call out. As they glided closer again, he was about to tell her to wait at the bottom, but she launched into a vaguely apologetic story about a cut, an infected paw, which had developed into a more serious illness she didn't know how to pronounce. Before she'd finished, she'd been carried away again, too far away to be heard.

When did this happen? He thought as one body after another flooded past. He'd barely finished being a puppy. At the top, Tim waited for several minutes, convinced that—since this was Nicole's route to work—she'd be coming up again soon. After a series of minor collisions with successive commuters—all of whom clicked their tongues in disapproval—Tim began to get fidgety. Where was Nicole? He couldn't see her. And he was already late for work.

Taking a deep breath, Tim stepped back onto the escalator, trotting to the bottom as fast as he could whilst muttering apologies to those he knocked into. He arrived, gasping for breath; he bent over, placing his hands on his knees he looked up to his right and saw Nicole several metres into her ascent. She turned his way and jokily smacked her palm to her forehead as if she'd forgotten to buy something at the supermarket. An announcement about a delayed train drowned out whatever she had started yelling at him. He squinted hard, trying to read her lips but it was hopeless. "Wait there? Go there? I'm there?" His hand went to his pocket as he contemplated chasing her back up the stairs, but—after realising he'd forgotten his inhaler—he decided to wait. After all, she'd just observed him sprinting all the way down. It was Nicole's turn now.

More commuters tramped past punctuated by a couple of police officers, a man with a rucksack overflowing with wedding brochures, but no Nicole. No signal on Tim's phone. Where was she? It was blindingly obvious that he'd just exhausted himself. And she knew about his asthma. He'd mentioned it on their second date. Come to think of it, he realised, there was that time he'd walked Terence in torrential rain, bathed him afterwards, and Nicole hadn't shown appreciation for any of that. He thought about that time he came home to find his smartest shoes chewed to pieces because *someone* hadn't closed the kitchen door properly. He missed that soppy creature. Nicole had kept him because—she said—his new place had been too small. A clear mental picture of what happened coalesced in Tim's mind: Nicole had been reading a text message, failing to pay proper attention, when Terence—the dear little scamp—had stepped on a rusty nail on the back lane to the park.

Ten minutes had passed. Still, he absolutely refused to go up after her. Or to turn up at her office for the second time that year unannounced and seething. If she wanted to speak with him so badly, well, it was her job to get on the escalator and come to him. As the crowds dissipated, Tim stared at the hypnotic steps of the escalator disappearing, one by one, travelling back to the top. Actually, he would ask, no, *insist* that Nicole fetch Terence's old ball *and* leash right away. Maybe he could hold a simple memorial service on his next lunch break, burying poor Terence's few possessions in the park near work. He could borrow a spoon from the pantry to dig the hole. Fired up, having removed his tie, he got back onto the escalator and glared straight up ahead. Nicole passed on his right with an expression of pure fury.

# CARRIAGE

I'D just caught the last train out of the city. I hadn't wanted to wait around for a taxi in the dark and cold. And I couldn't afford a taxi anyhow. The train clattered loudly as it passed under a bridge. The lights dimmed, then flickered back to their full brightness again. In the brief moment between dark and light, I noticed shaved heads, muscle-packed t-shirts, and brawny arms that crawled with tattoos. There were now three more passengers. A trio of teenage boys had entered the previously empty carriage and despite the abundance of empty seats they decided to sit around me in such a way that getting out instantly became a problem.

The tallest boy leant forward, placing his elbows on his knees. After a few moments of peering at me silently, he asked for my wallet. He asked as casually as you might ask a stranger for the time or the name of the next stop. I shuddered. There was no guard, no alarm, and certainly no way I could fight my way out. After a few more moments of silence, the boy repeated himself more gruffly, affecting an accent I'd heard on a popular TV show that month. "Mate. I said. Give. Us. Your. Wallet." One of the other boys had shoulders that could lift a reliable mid-sized family car with good mileage. The other, his biceps were covered in foreign scripture, and looked no less powerful. As the train swayed, oblivious, I remained silent. The leader, clearly displeased, got to his feet and shouted. "I said, *give me your fuckin' money.*"

I replied with the most fluent fake Russian I could manage.

"*Da, ik chin kring goski da stravinka na da.*" It was complete nonsense, but I hoped my tar-thick accent would prove convincing. I had long firmly held the belief that everyone is a little bit afraid of Russians. Even skinny, bookish Russians have a hardness about them that, in my opinion, no other nationality can quite muster. Taking his seat once more, the leader looked a little confused. "What's that, mate? English? Do ya speak English?" It didn't seem plausible, on a train in the middle of a country where English is the official language, not to know a single word. "Russian," I said, channelling a mouth full of gravel and vodka with a smattering of gruelling military training in inclement weather. "Russian," I said again, more proudly, jerking my thumb, once, decisively toward my chest.

The leader chuckled, shaking his head as if to give up. A small rush of relief was ruined, however, when he turned to his egg-headed-tattoo-covered companion: "Oi, Kristov, tell him to hand over his wallet yeah?"

Kristov nodded then stood, eyeing me gravely. "*Janovich mit Brita das niki vlad von ming ka.*" I stared back at him carefully, without a single idea as to what he'd just said but knowing full well what he'd meant. A bead of sweat crept down the side of Kristov's forehead. His inky arms seemed to vibrate. Without a clue what to do I did the boldest thing I could think of. I yelled back, waving my arms as if neat vodka flowed through them: "*Nacht macht bacht ving vlad blad isto bvery kitvich Volga.*" With the others looking fairly alarmed at the turn our conversation had taken.

"*Kak vas boot mit vishka,*" Kristov yelled.

"*Kak vas moot vit mishka,*" said I.

Next his voice fell to a whisper. "*Da…?*"

"*Na…*" I responded.

Kristov sat down.

The long silence that followed was interrupted by an announcement: my station was next. It shook the leader I'd originally been speaking with out of his trance. "Well,

Kristov?" he piped up. "Tha fuck did he say?"

"He said," Kristov answered, catching my eye for a brief moment, "that if we touch him his uncle is going to have our throats removed." Kristov paused, chewing his tongue. "I asked him which gang. He told me. Better leave this."

Keeping my gaze steady, I saw the leader fidget with the bezel on his watch. After a quick glance around the carriage, he snorted, got up and led the others to the next compartment. Kristov, shoulders rounding, hung back a little. Turning, he gave me a little nod. I broke into a smile that he returned for a moment, before he heard his name being called and his wrinkly skull passed out of my sight. I removed my book from under my leg and waited for my stop.

# ACCUMULATOR

**R**OY had made it through three rounds without using his Bonus Buster or halving his Credits in the Surprise Spinner. Even the usually uninterested camera crew were standing straight and watching him. He'd just knocked out Gregory, a PE teacher with an interest in karate, and absorbed his winnings too. Mercifully, the studio lights dimmed and the Host, Phil Crispin, wiped his forehead. "You sure know your African cities, Roy! I have to admit I didn't know half of those answers!"

A make-up artist ran up to Roy and he spoke between the soft strokes of her brush.

"Well, my wife, Judy, and I have been revising a lot, you see. After dinner we do half an hour of random topics from the encyclopaedia."

"That's marvellous! A real team! Is she in the audience tonight?"

A few seconds later a man in a black t-shirt appeared guiding a star-struck woman in heels. "You're doing so well, baby! I said you would!"

"We've never had a contestant do so well before, Judy," said Phil Crispin putting his arm around her waist. "What will you two spend the money on?"

Roy frowned, he was cautious and didn't want Judy to think he'd *definitely* win the jackpot but he had no complaint about them sharing the winnings. She'd helped him so much, after all. "Oh, I don't know. A hot tub or pool."

"They sound grand, Judy, how about a break? Any place either of you haven't been yet?"

"Oh, I don't know about that yet."

"What about study, become a student again!"

"Oh maybe—my Roy loves quizzes—I doubt there is anything he needs to study!"

Phil Crispin gave a polite laugh. "How about a fast sports car to drive around the city?" he said, pointing to a bright red convertible just offstage—the Bonus Prize. "Oh, sure, for *me* maybe. Roy can't drive."

Phil Crispin smoothed the small of her back. "Well, I'm pretty sure you'll be able to afford some lessons!" The lights came back on and Judy was ushered away. The theme music kicked in and the APPLAUSE sign flashed. "Welcome back!" shouted Phil Crispin to camera one. Half a dozen models in leather skirts paraded past with multitudes of cash in briefcases. "Well, Roy, who would you share this with? Is there a special woman at home?"

"Why, yes, actually my wife, Judy: she's been supporting me in my trivia hobby, ever since we walked down the aisle."

"Oh really?" teased Phil Crispin. "Perhaps we should get her down here to take your place?" Roy laughed but then became solemn. "She has been a rock for me." Camera 3 moved in for a close up on Judy's tearful eyes.

"That's lovely," said Phil Crispin, as his podium rose four metres. "I wish you the best of luck."

"Now, to win the accumulated funds in these briefcases you need to answer the questions from the computer's random topic. Or you can DEFECT with the kitchen unit and surfboard." A drum roll began. Roy looked at Judy who nodded. "ACCUMULATE!" confirmed Roy and the audience erupted into applause and cheers.

The big screen flashed categories at lightning speed: Latin Verbs, Living Nobel Prize Winners, Dog-Training Techniques, Japanese Island Culture, The Titanic, Moons in the Solar System—all leading to the life-changing Jackpot.

Roy slammed the button and his category was selected: 'Driving Test Criteria since 1965,' froze on the screen. Phil Crispin gave an enormous smile. "Good luck, Roy—do it for Judy," he winked.

# FLAT

STACEY stroked my hand as I shifted into fourth and drove us down the country lane. In the rear-view mirror, I could see her intimidating father, now snoozing like a tipsy bear, resting his head against the window. "You drive well, Jonathan," said Stacey's mum through the darkness over my shoulder. I thanked her and Stacey stroked my hand again. Relief washed over me. I had won her approval at least. My own mum had said it's all that really mattered because men his age would wait at least two decades before complimenting another man, and even then, it would be brief retrospective praise after six pints while climbing into a taxi.

I would ask Stacey to marry me before the year was through, and the twinkle in her mum's knowing eye at dessert had revealed it had crossed her mind. Just as I leaned across to kiss Stacey on the cheek, I was interrupted by a loud crash and slammed on the brakes. Something rolled off the bumper. "What the bloody hell was that?" shouted Stacey's father, now back to his surly ways and reaching protectively for his daughter.

Moments later we were gathered in front of the headlights forming shadows over the shallow respirations of a baby deer. "Can't you drive in the dark?" muttered Mr Surly as he began shepherding the women back into the car, trying to obscure their view with his large hands. I offered no response. The fawn's eyes were wide open. Mr Surly returned to survey the blood and feel the deer's neck.

"I'm not sure I can do much," he said through his teeth, stifling some blood which was oozing from its throat. He looked up at me somewhat helplessly. "Open the boot, Jonathan," he said, staring at me for a few moments. For the first time since we'd met, we shared a moment of understanding. I nodded and paced, as if in ceremony, back towards the rear of the vehicle whilst he comforted the helpless creature.

I moved their luggage and, rifling through my toolbox, I found a large spanner. I gripped it tightly and glanced over the car, catching sight of Mr Surly's breath pillowing confident clouds into the cold night air.

No matter how accidental, the horror of the fawn's suffering had scarred their impression of my suitability for their daughter. Thinking of my first dog, I knew I had to show I was a man.

I slammed the boot and strode back purposefully. I raised my weapon high and brought it down fast on the animal's tiny brittle skull, my vision blurring in a red mist. "What the hell are you doing?" cried Mr Surly, yanking the bloody tool from my hand. "My black bag, you damned fool! Surely my daughter told you I'm a vet?"

# SOAR

**A**S the students at St Andrew's Primary School got older they were encouraged to think a little more about what they wanted to become. A 'Careers Specialist' with a wacky education van arrived with comic strips, graphics and files bursting with information about the world of opportunity that lay before them. "You know kids, you can do anything you want if you work hard enough!" he yelled as he handed out the fun packs.

"I want to be an astronaut!" cried out nine-year-old Charlie. The Specialist chuckled as he clocked the boy's inhaler. Students drew pictures of where they saw themselves in twenty years' time. Jason drew himself as a kung fu action star. Marvin, a lawyer in a skyscraper. Bobby drew himself flying through the sky. "Do you want to be an astronaut? Find other planets for us to live on?" asked the Specialist.

"No," said Bobby, "I want to fly through the sky without a machine."

The Specialist ruffled the boy's hair and moved on to the next group who were madly drawing firefighters. At the end of the day, their efforts were displayed in a collage at the school reception. The Headmaster, joining the kids for a photo, shook the Specialist's hand vigorously. "You young stars must all come back and visit St Andrew's in a couple of decades, and I'll show you these pictures. If I'm still alive!"

The camera flashed and their dreams were set in film forever. The Specialist collected his cheque and drove away in his Careers Classroom Van. The kids ran out to play. Some of them pretended to be police officers or brave soldiers battling in a war. Bobby climbed to the top of the bike shed and stood proudly, focusing on the sky. Several of the other boys threw gravel at him.

# RUMMAGE

**R**ACHEL had warned how easy it is for someone like me to get lost wandering the streets of Tokyo. In fact, that's why she'd refused to come. She much preferred beaches. City breaks with a backpack were, according to Rachel, for students finding themselves, not serious couples who were in love like us. I was determined to prove her wrong.

Despite being captivated by the lights, dizzied by the language and somewhat inspired by the sheer variety of everything so alien to me, I was also tired and hungry, and I wanted to be back in my egg-sized hotel room. Maybe Rachel had been right in some respects.

As rush hour quietened down, I found myself second-guessing my decision to decline a comfortable and predictable stay at a resort with Rachel. Standing at the roadside, drenched in sweat and clutching the address of my hotel, I tried to calmly visualise the route I'd taken that morning. I seemed to have forgotten where I'd begun. I'd covered miles on foot. Now, with legs aching and stomach empty, at least my camera was filled with photos intended to prove to Rachel that I had made the right decision.

The taxis were enticing but eye-wateringly expensive. Desperate for my bed and English-language television, I reached what appeared to be the *same* sushi bar for the fourth time that day, I threw my arms up in frustration. As I lowered them, I found an elderly gentleman was feebly clutching my elbow. The bespectacled man dressed in ragged clothing was definitely Japanese and quite possibly over one hundred years old. He took the paper in my hand, frowning as he read the Westernised kanji several times. Then, nodding that he understood, he tapped me with his walking stick and started to amble in the opposite direction from which I'd come. Although he had yet to even look me in the eye, I took to mean that I was to follow him.

My knees were beginning to throb as we walked at his achingly slow pace. But I did not complain and I kept my mouth shut. He was so focused on his journey. He stopped several times to catch his breath. When I began to show signs of concern, he gestured decisively for me to step back.

After thirty minutes winding through a succession of thoroughly unfamiliar back streets, I was outside my hotel. It can't have been more than half a kilometre from where he'd found me. Smiling with relief, I watched as he pulled a few stray coins from his grubby pocket and slotted them into a glowing vending machine. It ejected a bottle of ice-cold water which he then offered to me. When I tried to show it wasn't necessary, he insisted by thrusting it towards me. I swear he was now yen-less. He bowed me goodbye and started to hobble away. Reaching into my own wallet, I tried pushing banknotes I'd changed at the airport into his hands, but he just let them flutter to the ground.

His footsteps as he hobbled away were so light, the street stayed perfectly silent. My eyes welling up in disbelief, I lifted my camera and focused on his bent back receding into the streetlamp gloom. I pressed the button a few times, knowing these would be outstanding quality. I even took a photo of the water bottle, focusing on the droplets that still clung to the surface. These would show Rachel, with absolute certainty, the full scope of the amazing experience she had missed. What sort of an all-inclusive beach resort would permit such priceless moments of human connection? Answer me that, Rachel. Don't you want more depth to our thirty-year wedding anniversary? I would explain to her that, sometimes, in a language barrier, there was a beauty to be uncovered. When I glanced down the street again, the old man was almost out of sight. I could just make out his grey hair, his shabby coat, the cane he carried, and the thick stream of urine as he pissed against a wall.

# CATCH

**M**AX stared at Josephine's phone number for over five minutes. He was back at his little flat sitting on the edge of his bed. It was almost 2am but he wasn't tired or drunk. He was simply elated; he'd finally got her number.

Three weeks ago, Max had been at the bar he usually stopped at after work. It served craft beer and chips apparently made of avocado. He'd noticed a woman closing the little gallery across the road and asked the barman about her. "Oh, that's Josephine, she just bought that place. She comes in from time to time," he said with a smile. Max felt himself blush. He thought Josephine was beautiful, a bit quirky perhaps. Financially independent. His kind of girl.

The next night Max had waited at the bar and when she'd come in he'd smiled and nodded at her in an unthreatening way, a gesture he'd practised in the mirror. Fortunately, she'd responded in kind and even added a little wave.

A week later, Max had hovered  by the windows of her gallery, looking quizzically at the paintings, hoping she'd come out to chat. But when she did, she'd asked what he thought of Chagall, and his mind was empty. Eventually he'd mumbled something about trying to draw a horse when he was six; it had looked like a lobster. Josephine giggled. Max, filling with tentative confidence, asked, "Fancy a beer later? I'll be at that bar."

Before she could answer, the phone inside the gallery had rung; she'd apologised and disappeared. Max was left feeling daft, wondering what on Earth had possessed him to mention the horse-lobster.

That night he waited at the bar, forcing himself not to stare at the doorway and trying to look casual as he tore 18 napkins to shreds. Two gin & tonics later he'd been well on his way to being drunk when Josephine walked in. Nerves had overwhelmed him; he'd only been able to gesture at the bar and smile awkwardly.

"So" Josephine had said "you're not an artist."

All Max had been able to do was reach into his rucksack and take out a stack of yellowing papers covered in crayon drawings. He'd felt her watching as he shuffled through them.

"Erm, did you want to show me something?" she'd said.

He'd held up the one he had been looking for right up to her face, too close. She'd taken half a step back and gently unpeeled his fingers from the paper.

"What am I looking at here? Is that a frog?"

Max had shaken his head.

"Oh, that's the lobster-horse you told me about!"

Max had nodded.

"And does the artist of this masterpiece have a name?"

Four artisanal beers, two portions of sustainably-sourced fish and chips, and one ethically harvested cold-brew coffee served in a vacuum flask later, Max had been chatty, rosy-cheeked, and confident. Which was why he'd felt so surprised when Josephine suddenly checked her watch, pecked his cheek, and made a swift wordless exit for the last bus home.

Max had been so confused and crestfallen, the barman had burst out laughing. "Cheer up, mate. When you were in the toilet, she asked me to give you this." He handed over a coaster with a phone number on it.

So now Max was sitting on the edge of his bed. He hadn't felt this apprehensive since the overly prudent colonic irrigation he'd had two days before a long-haul flight. He looked at Josephine's number again. She had a slanting hand with curls like an elf's shoes at the end of her 9s. An artist for sure.

At a pub the next day Max's friends held what felt like an international summit to discuss the issue. The pub landlord had even turned off the jukebox so that some old men at the other side of the room could offer their opinions. They agreed he should wait *three* days before calling.

When the third day came, *he* felt it was too soon. His pulse quickened as he started to punch in her number. He could feel his voice going up several octaves. It was bound to come out as a prepubescent squeak. He stopped right away and locked the coaster in his desk.

At lunch on Sunday, his mates asked how the first date had gone. Max revealed that he had yet to call. "Playing it cool for once, I like it," said one. They all cheered, reaching over and slapping his back vigorously. One or two squeezed his shoulder and he winced. He couldn't help but smile at their thoughtful support.

Max spent the next day drawing mind maps of potential greetings and topics for subsequent conversation. Nerves overwhelming him, he disguised himself in hat and glasses, before going for a brisk walk to calm down. The last thing he wanted was Josephine to see him before he actually called her. It would be artless.

Over Easter weekend, the following month, Max ended his tenancy prematurely and found a flat and a new job three hundred miles away. This was without a doubt, the coolest he had ever played it. He placed the coaster in an old photo frame next to his bed and the edges slowly yellowed in the sunlight.

That Christmas, Max almost gave in by calling Josephine

to wish her a merry time, but he distracted himself with port and cheese. He had to play hard to get.

Three years later, he was married to a beautiful barmaid from Barcelona called Graciela. She had curly hair and taught him Spanish on their patio in the evenings. Max moved Josephine's phone number to a small file where he kept his financial documents. He ignored it, knowing that not only would it be unfaithful to call Josephine but also a little too keen.

As Graciela and Max watched their son in his parade at the Naval Academy, they shed happy tears, but divorce came not long after. They both acknowledged that they cared for each other, but all that held them together was their boy. They stayed in touch and the following summer Graciela found a man who worked for coffee plantations and had hairier arms than Max.

Max returned to being a bachelor, and at the end of that decade he retired. At his retirement party he made a speech thanking his team and highlighting patience as the most important ingredient of his success.

Living off his pension, he had more free time. He managed his gout with a careful diet. His bilingual grandchildren visited most holidays, and he tickled them when they tried to steal his hat.

Gardening one day, Max felt tightness as if a hundred hammers were pressing down on his chest. A few weeks on a large white bed saw him right again but he had to take it easy. He took medication and carried a cane or else, the doctor threatened a pacemaker would follow swiftly.

One evening, after asking his kindly neighbour to fetch a box from his attic, Max fished out the folder containing Josephine's telephone number. The name of the bar he had frequented was almost invisible but her number, in black pen, was still there. He grew nervous, wondering if he should take any more pills before he made the call. A few moments later, he could hear her phone ringing. A childish voice answered with glee.

"Hello there," said Max "I was wondering if a lady by the name of Josephine lives there?"

The child giggled. There was some commotion and a second, more mature voice came on the line,

"Hello, sorry my daughter loves playing with the phone."

Max repeated his question.

"Oh, I'm afraid Mum had an early night tonight. But I'm sure she can call you back tomorrow. May I ask who is calling?"

Max smiled confidently

Tell her it's Max. The man with the horse-lobster. She'll know who."

He gave his number, wished her daughter a good evening and hung up.


Max's friends from the pub years ago would have slapped his back and pinched his skin at how cool he'd played it. Josephine now had *his* number. The ball was firmly in her court. He wouldn't try again tomorrow. He wouldn't consider wandering past her house or looking her up on this new thing called social media. No, quite rightly, now it was all down to her.

# ODDS

"NO. 4 to win," Charles said to the stranger standing next to him. The stranger looked down at his betting slip and considered his options again—he had no idea. He'd chosen based on the colour of the jockey's jersey (red went faster). Thrown into uncertainty by the anonymous tip, he furiously ripped up his ticket. "Tough isn't it?" observed Charles, unflustered by the tantrum.

"Yes."

"Don't bet then," said Charles. "I don't, I haven't bet on a horse in years, but I gamble all the time."

The stranger patted his pockets, suddenly convinced this was all a ruse to steal his wallet. Charles noticed and chuckled. "I'm just dispensing wise advice so you can have a good time—all the thrill but no losing that money you worked for." Perplexed, the stranger continued to listen to Charles who was, a man who guessed the outcome of everything: horses, greyhounds, dice, and the timing of traffic lights, but never laid down a penny. Charles asked him to compare the excitement of laying down half a month's wages on a horse coming up a yard behind in the final furlong with the torment of *not* betting on it and praying it didn't win.

The two men stood and watched the horses gallop. Both clutched betting slips on which neither had laid a wager, yelling for their favourite to lose. "Thank goodness I didn't choose that one," panted the stranger, elated when Hooves of Fury unseated his four-foot-tall ginger jockey.

"The night has just begun," announced Charles. The stranger, now a friend, went back to Charles's grotty little home and sat in front of the secondhand TV set.

"I didn't lose a penny," said Charles to his desperate-looking wife who'd just returned from work. The two men sat in the living room with a crate of beer, crossing their fingers as they stared in rapture at the TV, praying their lottery numbers wouldn't be drawn.

# APPRECIATION

**P**ROFESSOR Wardly lost his wife to old age. He took a year's sabbatical from his tenured position teaching English to grieve. Unable to contemplate anything from the past that held the memories of his true love and fellow critic, Wardly tried to develop new interests in popular culture.

After becoming disgusted by modern men's magazines, appalled by contemporary cinema, and sickened by recent novels, he turned his attention to radio. He tuned in to a local station, seeking refuge, when he stumbled across a new song by Mindy Tinger, a 17-year-old American with a guitar and long socks.

'Freeze my Love' was an acoustic ballad mixed with synthesised drums which had been at number one for the last ten weeks. The song faded out and was replaced by an enthusiastic DJ muttering into his mic. Professor Wardly opened his eyes and found himself curled on the floor in the foetal position. He'd quite lost track of himself. Something in her voice had reached deep inside him.

Wardly bought the song and listened to it whenever he felt a wave of grief. It was better than any counselling, advice, or visit from a neighbour or ex-student. He wanted to find the artist and thank her personally. She'd saved him from perpetual mourning.

Clutching his ticket, Wardly took his seat at the back of the concert venue. A sea of heads jumped about in front of him, obscuring his view almost completely. When the song— his song—was sung, he could barely hear it over the noise of the crowd. Feeling disappointed, he left early to secure a place among the throngs already gathered at the stage door.

After an hour of squirming and squeezing, he'd fought his way through all the screaming teenagers and reached the front. When Mindy appeared, the surge of writhing bodies almost bent him in half over the barricade. He thrust an old photo of his wife out towards Mindy. Cameras flashed, paparazzi shouted, and high-pitched squeals seemed to be interfering with his hearing aid. He caught Mindy's eye and she wandered over, swathed in a cloak of bodyguards.

"What ya got here?" she yelled past a hundred arms reaching out to her.

"My wife!" he called back, ribs crushed against the barricade. "She passed away, I was broken. Your song helped me so much!"

"What?" shouted Mindy, who couldn't hear a word the old man was saying.

She and her equally deafened aides shrugged. She took the photo and scrawled 'love Mindy' over his wife's face in thick pink marker pen.

"Thanks for coming," said Mindy, patting his outstretched hand before clambering into her limousine. The car drove off with dregs of the crowd chasing hopelessly behind.

The remaining fans turned to Wardly and screamed with jealousy. "She signed it! She never signs *anything*!"

"How much do you want for it?" yelled a beefy guy in a trench coat and glasses. He was at least thirty years older than the teenagers around him. Wardly looked down at the photo with Mindy's autograph barely legible except for a heart above the 'i'.

Dozens of teenagers were now enveloping him, trying to get a glimpse of the signature. "She touched you!" shouted one young acne-covered boy in a hoody. "I'd kill for that."

The beefy guy was growing impatient. Thrusting a wad

of notes into Professor Wardly's top pocket, he snatched the photo away. He marched through a wall of jealous cries as if he were a large gorilla through tall grass.

"What did her hand feel like?" asked one fan breathlessly. Before Wardly could even think about responding, another yanked his sleeve. "It was his right hand, here. Look, I think you can see some of her makeup."

"Let me see!" yelled another. In seconds they were tugging at Wardly in a frenzy, shouting and swearing about how lucky he was to have come so close to their beloved.

# QI

"WHAT, you wore one of those orange robe things and shaved your head?" questioned the second-prettiest one. "Well, no," Jason said, frustrated once again that his best mate had brought up the topic of his trip to learn kung fu in China as an icebreaker with girls.

"Show us a move then," said the prettiest one.

"Nah, look, now isn't the right time." Jason glared at Matt who grinned as he glanced at their chests.

"Come on Jay, I haven't seen anything yet." A flat-out lie coupled with a barely concealed smirk. But the girls didn't know him and took it at face-value. They looked on in anticipation. After hesitating, Jason took off his shoes, tucked them under his bar stool, rolled up his sleeves, and performed a sequence of moves from the White Crane style. His strange, swift, precise punches and kicks sounded like a tea towel being whipped, drawing raised eyebrows and giggles from the girls.

"You could protect me if you did that?" said the prettiest one with her red wine-stained teeth. She touched Jason's arm, the balmy scent of alcohol diffusing around her. Matt held his breath and looked at her chest again. "It isn't about that," Jason proclaimed. "It is as much an art as it is a way of life."

She drew back her fists and did some shadow boxing: a jab here and there and a duck of the head. A few men raised their pints and cheered. Matt shouted encouragement and stared at her bare waist. "Show him what you're made of!"

Jason, observing the audience that had begun to watch, put up his hands and gestured that she should calm down. She jabbed again, only this time her ring caught his lip which bled immediately and sent a bolt of adrenaline to course through to his fists. "Enough," Jason exhaled, wincing with indignity. He snapped his hand out with the speed of a cobra and pulled her wrist down towards him. She fell forward into his arms smiling. "Woah," she swooned, oblivious to his left foot performing a gentle but efficient hooked leg sweep which tilted her back in conflict with her now trapped wrist. Her shoulder popped immediately out of its socket, its delicate sound muting the room.

# BULBS

"WE'LL see," she said and hung up rather suddenly. It was very dark, and the bench Dave was sitting on smelt of urine. But things weren't as grim as he had thought. If she wanted space, he would give it to her. Time, that had also been mentioned. He would give her that too. It was 2am. He shivered. Tuxedos looked warmer than they actually were; with red wine poured down the front the deposit being returned seemed unlikely. Even more unlikely if it smelt of dog piss.

The air was crisp and silent except for the dying bulb of a streetlamp buzzing above him. Why hadn't it been replaced? How did people know when to change them? Surely *all* the bulbs would go at the same time? They must have all been installed together when the housing estate was built. The logic of the world—it made him laugh out loud.

He called Katie to tell her. He was chuckling as she answered the phone. He described his observation about the bulbs and how strange it was they ran out at different times. Why hadn't the factory implemented some sort of longevity scheme or quality control system—he wasn't sure of the precise term but he was sure Katie would know what he meant.

Katie explained she was tired and *really* needed space— from silly ideas at stupid o' clock in the morning; from embarrassing arguments about petty jealousy at friends' weddings; from bulbs provided by council estates to light public pathways; from him. She hung up after telling him not to contact her for at least another week.

"Council estates, eh?" he thought. "I'll write to the council and tell them a bulb needs replacing. I'll tell them my idea too!"

He opened the front door quietly so as not to wake his parents. Using the house phone, he called Katie one more time. After a couple of rings, he got her answer machine. "I love you," he said. "You're an inspiration."

Dave drafted a letter to the council suggesting they synchronise the installation of their light bulbs to save on maintenance call-out fees or to contact their production facility. He didn't expect payment for his idea but acknowledgement in a local newspaper or gazette would have been appreciated. He thought about the light bulbs again and his plan to rescue Katie from her silly, wobbly concerns about their relationship. She was overreacting. He soon slept and dreamt of waning filaments, but not before he set his alarm for 6am. He wanted to be up and ready when the petrol station got its delivery of fresh flowers.

# CRACKS

I T was Jessie's idea that we wore matching clothes on the first day of our honeymoon. She pulled the outfits out of a compartment I didn't know we had in our suitcase and threw mine at me. As we walked hand-in-hand to the complimentary beachside breakfast I saw everybody else here was dressed like a performing circus twin too, so I tried to forget about it.

There was a cool breeze coming across the open plan restaurant and a luscious array of fruits, breads, and omelette fillings on display. The waiter's English was excellent. With a little bow he acknowledged our first morning as husband and wife with some cool champagne. He smiled at my pink shorts and said I looked very much in love. I ordered a strong coffee and Jessie commented that I should probably eat something first before filling my body with so much caffeine. She changed my order and soon a watermelon juice was sitting in front of me.

Jessie again made some observations about Paul's Best Man speech; she'd thought it was a little lewd and she hadn't appreciated him sharing his initial impression that she was 'bossy'.

I didn't speak. It was bothering me that she hadn't brushed her teeth yet. We'd had a chat about morning-breath some time ago. Our food arrived and as I took my first bite of matrimonial toast I was interrupted by an old guy seated behind me; I'd seen him holding his wife's wrinkly hand when we sat down.

"We sat here on our first day too. Of course, back then this was barely a resort, let alone a five-star one." Jessie and

I turned to face them. The old guy kissed his wife's hand and she did a little smile with her few remaining teeth. The couple looked old, so old, I guessed they'd retired before I was born.

I took in their gold jewellery, their crisp linen shirts, and the pot of hand cream beside her cutlery.

"How long have you two been married?" piped up Jessie, her mouth full of bacon.

They answered in unison, "Seventy years and one day!" She nuzzled her husband's shoulder like an affectionate horse. Despite my headache and apparently sour mood that morning, I couldn't help but admire them. They certainly seemed successful. This resort wasn't cheap.

"What's your secret?" I asked, feeling embarrassingly childlike.

"Olive oil, fine wine, and sex," said the husband with a teasing wink. They dropped their napkins on the table, stood up and ambled away. The old husband smacked his wife's arse with a resounding clap, then squeezed it 'til his entire hand disappeared from view.

Jessie kicked my shin. "If you do that to me when we leave here then you can sleep in the hammock."

I sat back and ordered the strongest coffee known to man, carefully planning the accident that would spill it on our matching t-shirts.

# BONUS

**S**ARAH won the triple rollover lottery draw 18 hours after we'd finishing signing the official papers at the solicitor's office. Our marriage was over. My friends showed me a video of Sarah on the news. She was holding a big cheque and the guy from the gym was spraying her with champagne.

"You're much better off without her, anyway," said Gary. The others nodded in agreement. Although we were seated around the circular plastic garden furniture that was now my dining table. None of them looked me in the eye.

I followed Sarah's exploits online. She became a relative celebrity, using a portion of her winnings to launch an eye-catching clothing brand. The profits helped disabled kids in our area pay for their textbooks. When interviewed about her love life, Sarah never mentioned my name or the struggles we'd had since we walked down the aisle. The principle issue had been both of us working full-time to save for a garage extension, yet it was never mentioned. Sometimes we'd only talk to each other by the sink as we brushed our teeth before bed. It had turned us stale.

One evening, I'd been in a ratty mood because, once again, there was nothing in the fridge and Sarah hadn't bought milk or reminded me to. I'd suggested a short break from each other, and she'd quickly agreed. By Halloween it had escalated into a perfectly amicable separation with almost no tears. Sarah began taking exercise more seriously. As we moved her stuff to her parents' place, I'd noticed how easily she lifted the boxes. Now, having correctly predicted seven numbers, Sarah had acquired a special bank account and a new phone line.

When I looked up her winning numbers, I was startled

to discover that one was my birthday month, and another was the date we'd got engaged. Further investigation revealed that the Bonus Ball was derived from the name of a restaurant we'd visited on our honeymoon. I sent a home-made Christmas card to her new house, which was actually more like a small castle. Aside from my festive wishes I asked if she fancied 'catching up' in the New Year and made a joke about her feet. I signed with my full name, which I regretted a few moments after putting it in the post-box.

A few weeks later, Sarah picked me up in a flashy sports car. We went to The Quay where all the staff seemed to know her. She ordered for me (knowing exactly what I'd like) and I noticed my back muscles relaxing. When it came to drinks the waiter automatically handed Sarah his pen and held up the menu like a target. She closed her eyes and threw it at the list of beverages. It made a small mark next to lime soda. The waiter nodded, picked up the pen and walked to the bar.

"What did you do that for?!" I chuckled, suddenly missing her arbitrary silliness.

"Oh, that's how I chose my lottery numbers. It worked well for me then, so you never know what'll happen next! Luck is blind, Jeremy!" Her phone rang and she answered with a radiant smile, nodding, and confirming something with cute little 'uh huh' sounds. Holding the phone between her ear and shoulder she reached into her handbag for an extremely expensive-looking fountain pen, thick cream paper embossed with her maiden name, and a calculator. These she placed one-by-one on the table in front of her. After hanging up the phone to someone called Frankie, who could have been a man or a woman, I suppose—she apologised then wrote my name, underlining it twice. "Right so, Jeremy, I want to help you with that 'fridge fullness and milk quantity detector' you mentioned a while back."

I gave a little chuckle and told her I had, of course, been joking when I was a little frustrated; it was, most likely, due to my own oversight about who should be buying milk. Sarah quickly interrupted me,

"Oh no, Jeremy, you mentioned it quite often and I think it was a really good idea so, just throw me the basics, I'm sure you've had time to develop it. Oh, and a budget! Let's see if I can get my team to work something up with you."

# RUB

THE wizened genie appeared, an irritated look on his face.

"Oh wow! A real genie!" yelled Glen, suddenly forgetting his blistered hands after digging for treasure at the beach all morning.

With all the enthusiasm of an aging horse about to climb a spiral staircase, the magical being ran through the various rules and stipulations of the three wishes it would grant.

"Gee," said Glen, his sweaty, acne-covered face now stretched into a beaming smile, "I'd sure like a better body, clear skin, and straight teeth—that way Mary-Beth will finally take notice of me for sure!"

Although Glen's wish technically incorporated several desires, the Genie waved its arm and granted them. A few seconds later Glen had transformed into a far more socially acceptable boy. He threw the lamp in his bag and strutted home with his bulging new quadriceps.

The following evening, Glen complained to the bored Genie that although he'd received plenty of compliments from classmates and even teachers, Mary-Beth had paid him no attention. She'd just sat quietly in the corner with her book.

The genie shrugged and gestured that Glen should hurry up and make his second wish. A puff of smoke later, Glen had more pocket money than he could hold in his rucksack.

The following day, he bought everyone in the school snacks from the tuck shop and took everyone ice-skating. But Mary-Beth didn't enter the rink. Instead, she sat in the spectator stand drawing pictures of cats, oblivious to Glen's flexing muscles as he skated tight circles on the ice in front of her.

"I don't get it, Genie! Why don't you meet her and see what you think I should do? Then I can know for sure." The Genie breathed heavily through its nose announcing this was not the 'done thing' but consented when Glen agreed to polish the inside of the lamp.

On the bus Glen snuck next to Mary-Beth and showed her his lamp. The Genie appeared but she expressed no surprise. "Oh, you again," she said venomously, "I thought I'd buried you deep enough in the sand."

Glen was dumbfounded. "You know her?" he cried. The Genie nodded and said Mary-Beth had found the lamp some weeks ago. She'd also been disappointed with the outcomes of her wishes. "What did you ask for?" asked Glen, no longer so self-conscious. Mary-Beth glared at the Genie as she spoke: "A new bike, better drawing skills, and a boyfriend who wasn't going to behave like a kid all the time by pulling my hair if he liked me."

The Genie looked at the ceiling. The bus went over a speed bump. There was a long silence. "Well, now you know why Mr Cavill was fired," said Mary-Beth with an impatient huff. They all got off the bus a few stops early and headed straight for the farmyard.

Glen demanded his final wish be that everything be turned back to normal.

The Genie became more attentive. "What are you going to do?"

"Grant my wish!" shouted Glen and instantly his car-wreck smile, greasy skin, and empty wallet returned. He took a handful of cow muck and shoved it in the lamp so hard that bits started coming out of the spout. Mary-Beth helped too, giggling as the Genie disappeared into his new sticky brown world, gurgling for mercy. "There, Mary-Beth, that's done it," he said after dropping it into a septic tank.

"Thank you, Glen," said Mary-Beth, beaming.

"You know my name?" burst Glen, delighted.

"Of course I know your name, Glen Mattersby. If only you'd come over to chat instead of staring." They turned and walked towards the bus stop, their filthy, shit-caked fingers entwined.

# TALES

**M**ELANIE usually looked miserable. On the rare occasions she smiled though, she looked *stunning*. She wore gothic makeup and black clothes to her work at the local record shop. I bought vinyl I didn't need, just to be near her, to make her laugh, to see her face transform. It was a reward.

One day, I casually picked up a Phil Collins LP and made a joke about the film *American Psycho*. Melanie smirked. I leaned on the counter and delivered a short anecdote about my father who once accidentally played a Genesis hit mocking televangelism to his mother-in-law during a drive to church. Melanie exhaled and her lip started to quiver into a smile. She looked radiant for that glimpse of a moment. I asked her out for coffee the next day. She said, "Sure, whatever."

I waited on a worn leather chair at a café. Melanie moped in and I kissed her cheeks, like the French do. She didn't recoil. My friends had explained that if Melanie wasn't talkative I should tell her some more of my many excellent anecdotes. We ordered drinks and sat in silence while Melanie picked at her nails. I wanted her to smile.

There was a dachshund lying in a patch of sunlight, so I told Melanie about the dog I'd grown up with. "He used to bring the shopping in from the car, yeah? And we'd reward him only to find out that he'd been stashing microwave meals under the…"

Melanie had begun to look even more downcast.

"Sorry, that's a sweet story, but can we not talk about dogs, please. I had to have mine put down last month."

"Oh, I'm sorry, what happened?" I asked, feeling rather awkward.

"I don't want to talk about it, sorry."

Our coffee arrived and Melanie added five sugars without stirring. I smiled at the waitress for her. My eyes then settled on a tattoo just visible under Melanie's sleeve. It was a skull with a jaw wrenched open into a terrifying scream. I began reminiscing about a school trip to an exhibition of sarcophagi where my friend, Paul, had hidden in a recycling bin.

"I'm really sorry, I don't like hide and seek," said Melanie. "We played it once as kids. There was an ambulance in the driveway when I had finally given up on hiding in the bushes. My uncle had thrown himself off the roof and onto the new patio furniture because of a bad credit rating."

I was already beginning to understand why she never smiled. I reached out and touched her hand. "I'm so sorry," I said. "What would you prefer to talk about?"

"Tell me about what kind of tattoo you're going to get," she said, looking up.

"Erm, I'm not too sure about that to be honest. I'm scared of needles." I absolutely did not want a tattoo.

Melanie looked disappointed then stared into her cup miserably as if it contained liquid death.

"My doctor says I have a high chance of becoming a Type 2 diabetic."

I handed her my pen and a napkin.

"Hey, design me my first tattoo," I said.

"Really?" she blurted, beaming. My spine turned pleasantly cool.

I nodded and she quickly set to work. The sausage dog on the floor woke up. He looked at me, licking his little nose as if he'd dreamt about eating something tasty. Perhaps I could get a tattoo of my old dog. I had a photo of him somewhere still.

I glanced across and saw Melanie scribbling away. My napkin was now emblazoned with an enormous eagle dripping with broken hearts and used syringes. "For your back!" she said. That gorgeous smile stayed all day.

# PANTS

**M**ARVIN, a British man on secondment in a New York law firm, was having difficulty socialising. While his colleagues were friendly, they didn't seem to want to make friends and when he finished work, he saw the sights alone. He was very busy with work, often finishing after sunset, but he also felt his Britishness was a factor. He thought they must assume he was cold, unemotional, and a bit stuffy compared to their all-embracing American positivity and hearty, well-tipped meals.

He tried to be more relaxed at work; he even wore a baseball cap backwards to lunch. But it made no difference. After two months he was still the solitary one in the office and was considering an official complaint to Human Resources. People didn't knock on his office door with social invitations. He felt awkward, especially when he spoke, what with his accent standing out so much. He stopped drinking tea and ordered frappuccinos instead. He gave up on the BBC and began with checking basketball scores on the news. He softened his English, dragging out rhotic Rs at the water cooler. Still, nothing worked, and as New Year's Eve approached, Marvin was terrified of spending it alone in his *flat*, which he now called his *apartment*.

The night arrived and he hadn't received a single invitation. Marvin tossed his phone in the bin, which he now called a *trash can* and drunkenly hung around near the *elevator* from 4pm, watching the staff leave the office for the final time that year. He held a bottle of vodka in his hand just in case anyone wanted to invite him to a party. No luck. As the final group got into the lift, he joined them. As they began their descent, Marvin began to wonder why he was hated and ignored. He slammed his fist down on the emergency stop button, ripping open the panel and tearing out wires angrily.

Immediately the lift went dark. Yelps and screams echoed around the lift shaft. "Oh my gawd, Marvin! What the hell did you do?" After a few minutes, everyone had settled into the impenetrable darkness.

Marvin figured they'd all shifted to the opposite side.

He cleared his throat. "Now listen you lot," he said in his accent, which was crisper and clearer than ever. "There's a party tonight and I'm pretty sure none of you have invited me. Especially *you* guys. You haven't given me time of day at all. Even when I talk about basketball!"

There was a long silence and one of his younger female colleagues piped up.

"The guys aren't here, Marvin, they left at four. It's just me, Rachel, and the girls from accounting."

Marvin's jaw throbbed at the horror of his situation. "We expected you to organize a party. But you didn't. Gary is at Josh's place now."

Another girl spoke, her voice riddled with fear. "You've been the nicest Senior Partner we've ever had. You're so professional. You aren't in our faces all the time. We thought that was what you wanted. You let us do our jobs. Please don't hurt us."

One of them swallowed, then she cursed the lack of reception on her phone.

He started calling for help and banging on the door. The girls screamed. Marvin apologised profusely. An hour later he had to apologise again. He'd been forced to relieve himself in the corner. At midnight they all sat in silence, backs propped against the wall, and held their noses.

"If you listen really carefully," piped up Marvin in the spirit of camaraderie, "you can hear the fireworks outside."

# Impressions

**J**EFF greeted each student as they walked in. He didn't know their names yet, but he soon would. He promised himself he'd learn them as a sign of respect. It was a 'good' school. Well, it was one of the better ones in the area, but he'd still better be cautious. As each student entered, they looked him up and down. Sizing him up. He didn't want disciplinary issues on his first day. Jeff kept his stare firm but fair, and occasionally he pretended to make notes. His students found their seats without any fuss and got out their textbooks. Organised and quiet teenagers. Was this a prank? He exhaled in quiet relief.

Time to get started. He sat on the edge of his desk, his legs swinging casually. He'd practised this at home in front of the mirror.

English Literature was a cool class. Jeff looked cool.

He started off by telling them about his previous job as a lawyer and how the English language had been his *tool*. He was especially pleased with that choice of word. He elaborated in case they thought he meant a literal tool, like a spanner. *Language* was a tool, he explained, because it aided expression. *Language* was of critical importance to conveying any aspect of 'socially constructed identity' he or his students cared to name. It was vital they express themselves well. Even if they didn't love the books, they were going to study. Books were both a *tool* and a form of art. He was thrilled to use that word again: *tool*.

The students stared at him. Jeff could tell his fresh angle on teaching was being appreciated. So, he went onto describe various cases he had worked on and how the last one, a medical malpractice suit, had turned him to teaching. Suing hardworking doctors had seemed like the "fucking devil's work," explained Jeff. Some of their mouths fell open. He took a long pause and wandered over to the blinds. He knew he shouldn't swear but he needed to make his point clearly to these 13-year-olds. And now he could tell he had their attention. He'd impressed them.

Retracting his finger from between the shutters, Jeff strolled back to his desk and dragged out his chair. He sat on the edge with his fingers steepled against his nose as if devising a mind-boggling checkmate. He talked about the language of the law, deliberately throwing in words like 'fatuous', 'iridescent', and 'diaphanous policy-making' and glancing up at the ceiling as if his memories were painted there. Rumours of his laid-back, intelligent approach to teaching would spread through the school. His classes this term, and in terms to follow, would be easy, thanks to this first tranche of mature and responsible students. He remembered the dull teachers he had had decades ago and winced at their dry and uninspiring style.

The bell rang and the students filed out. A few girls giggled. Jeff still had his looks despite the grey hairs. He closed the door and as he returned to his desk, he realised his shoelace was undone. He bent down to tie it and immediately noticed a cool breeze on his groin. His flies were also undone. The gap in his underwear was confidently wide. The button had come free, parting like the Red Sea for Moses. Poking out between the fabric, with an air of pre-emptive apology, was the flaccid, crumpled tip of his penis. There could be absolutely no doubt that they'd all noticed.

He heard the classroom clock and his own heartbeat tick together. It had been a 35-minute class. He hadn't visited the bathroom since rushing out of the morning staff meeting.

There was a new silence in the corridor outside. Zipping himself up, Jeff gingerly approached the door. There didn't seem to be anything unusual on the other side of the thin pane of glass. Turning the handle, he opened it a crack so he could peer down the hallway.

The staircase outside was full of teenagers biting down on their lower lips to stifle any laughter. Apparently most of the school had assembled. After a few seconds, one of them spotted Jeff and called out. His eyes were met with instant howls, screams, wolf whistles, and party streamers.

Looking to make an escape in the other direction Jeff slipped through the door only to be greeted by another wall of students offering him high fives and chanting his Christian name, many of them reaching out with marker pens begging him to autograph student election posters that had been torn down and covered with hastily drawn baby serpents and dachshunds all smiling in anticipation of the year to come.

# CHAPTER

I SQUEEZED past a tearful man who was clutching a wreath, and took the window seat beside him. His floral arrangement filled most of the table. The woman sitting opposite didn't hide her irritation and I closed my eyes for a few minutes to escape the tension. When I opened them, the grieving man had gone and I took in the woman.

She was reading my book. This was the first time I'd seen someone reading it. I felt a burst of excitement. She turned a page and then rolled her eyes a moment later. Flicking to the next page after that, she seemed rather frustrated. Quickly, she skipped to the next, then the next, before slamming the book down on the table. She glared at the houses whizzing by outside.

"Not a good book?" I ventured with a smile.

"Sorry? What?" she said.

"You don't look too happy with that book," I said with a little laugh. "You didn't even bookmark the page you'd got to."

"Oh right," she said. "Yeah, well, I gave it a chance. But it's painfully predictable."

I winced, but also felt a bubble of confidence rise. The whole payoff of the book was the massive twist at the end. '*The twist that almost made me want to pick it up and read it again!*' one critic (a friend) had written. "Maybe it'll surprise you?" I said. "You're over halfway through. Seems a waste not to—"

"No. I skipped most of it. I hate train journeys. My car is in the garage and I left my other book at home by accident." She paused to glare at the book. "I can see where this is going. We think the narrator is in charge, but actually he's a prisoner. Probably has some mental delusion. Do you know what this cost? Bloody hardbacks."

Although she was getting really riled up, she was only half right about the ending.

"This is a nice train," I announced. She ignored me and continued her rant.

"I mean, really, if I'd been *given* this book, I wouldn't be so angry. But I'm not exactly loaded now the clutch has gone on my car. And now I'm hungry." She grabbed the book again and turned to the last few pages, scanning through them with an expression approximating an intern on their first day at the sewage works. "Oh, I wasn't far off!"

I then remembered that juxtaposed with the final line (*'Life is a prison if you only peer through the bars'*) was a black and white photograph of me holding a mug and looking out of a train window on a rainy day.

She stared at the book for a few more moments, squinting at it, and then me. I waited before I finally spoke. "I'm sorry, I should have told you I wrote it before. It's just…"

"No, *I'm* sorry," she interrupted. "But *you* should be sorry for writing such predictable nonsense." She snorted, but I was determined to persuade her with further thoughtful discussion.

"Then maybe I should buy you lunch?" I said, amazed at how smoothly I'd segued into flirting.

"Well, you do owe me a refund," she said. "I'm not even joking."

I leaned forward slightly so that the light would catch me like it had in my author photo. Looking at her ticket on the table next to her pen, I saw our destinations were the same. I couldn't have written this level of serendipity. Beaming, I took out my wallet and revealed my matching ticket.

"Yes, cash is fine," she said, fishing out a couple of my banknotes from my wallet. She pushed the book across the table to me. I looked down at the cover. An enticing image of mystery that had not delivered.

"As you seem to be going to the same place as me, perhaps I could also buy you lunch at Oak House Deli?" I said, stroking the embossed lettering I'd insisted on. I looked up. She'd already put her headphones on and was popping successive travel mints into her mouth. She was certainly a feisty one, but I decided a speech bubble on my author photo asking her about lunch would be irresistibly charming. I could push it under her nose like a school kid passing notes to his crush. Turning to the back page, I found the photo had been vandalised with a pair of silly glasses, a moustache, 'PRIZE PRAT' scrawled over my bowtie, and a hastily drawn screwdriver stuck in my forehead.

# ZEST

UNCLE Bernard said he'd already organised his own funeral. He knew he was dying. Everybody would roll their eyes and impatiently tell him it wasn't an appropriate topic in front of the children. They were tired of his jokes and cries for attention. My entire family agreed that Uncle Bernard had always been annoying. By the time I was born they'd lost all tolerance. He used to get out his banjo and try to start sing-a-longs at barbecues; he'd wake people at 3am with phone calls full of demented animal noises; he'd go up behind the nieces and nephews and wiggle his fingers in their ears as they ate ice cream.

Once, I heard my father call him a 'bloody nuisance manchild' but I actually rather liked Uncle Bernie's silly approach to life. He wasn't married, yet he seemed jollier than any of my cardboard-cutout family.

When we visited him at the hospital he'd pull 'magic' coins out from behind people's ears and try to keep them laughing; he'd pronounce their names backwards or pretend to be in a fighter jet as his blood was being taken.

My father had grown especially sick of Uncle Bernie's humour after the summer he'd bought a giant haystack to hide the keys to his new car; the first person to find them before sundown won a prize of fresh plums. All his elaborate attempts to get everyone together were rebuffed after that.

At his funeral we gathered to face the coffin. It was on a conveyor belt ready for cremation. I was the only who cried. My father read a poem off his phone that he'd looked up that very morning.

A neighbour, Mrs Lodge, came up to speak and explained

it was Uncle Bernie's dying wish that we all hear one of his new silly songs. Despite the occasion, I heard several groans. Mrs Lodge placed a CD in the player at the front and the familiar strumming of Uncle Bernie's banjo, slightly out of tune, filled the room. He began singing about a man who went to market and bought the wrong fruit; his wife had sent him out again but he kept forgetting what she wanted. Each verse featured a new fruit and the chorus got louder each time.

*"Oh silly Mr Arker, down the market he did go. He wanted to buy some fruit but what kind he did not know!"*

Occasionally Uncle Bernie shook a tambourine so it bashed into the microphone. By the eighth verse the coffin remained motionless, and the patient, polite smiles that everyone had been trying to use to rejoice the life of Bernard Wellington had disappeared. Fifteen minutes later a screech cut through the hall as the main door opened, revealing the confused faces of mourners from the next funeral. An usher appeared, whispering to the mourners in sympathetic tones before closing the door. Our heads turned back to the front and the song continued. Bernie was singing about how Mr Arker had bought cranberries and his wife was *still* mad at him.

There was another knock, and a woman in tears asked if this was the place where she was supposed to say goodbye to her husband. Uncle Bernie's song continued, and everyone's soft murmurs grew to a babble until my father stood up, sweating. "Thank you, all of you, for coming to say goodbye to my eccentric brother. Now I suggest we make way for the next party. Thank you."

We walked out under the frowns of close to 200 delayed mourners, many of them holding wreaths. My father muttered apologies before attempting a shortcut around some bushes.

Uncle Bernard jumped out. "Baby Brother!" he exclaimed,

all hearty and jolly. "You should have seen your face in there!" He turned to the rest of us as we took in his strap-on red nose, outsize shoes, and a broad, bright green tie that ran down to his knees. "Come on! You miserable lot! Don't worry, I'm here to cheer you up!"

Blowing his kazoo a couple of times, Uncle Bernie pointed across the road towards the grubby car park. Inside that car park next to my father's car, now stood a bright, multi-coloured bouncy castle and an ice-cream van playing its jaunty tune.

# DETAILS

I **ASKED** out the model from my life drawing class and she said yes.

I'd put away the pencils, which we'd had to buy at the start of the course, and rolled up my sheet to stash inside the long plastic tube, then I'd asked Megan if she wanted to grab a cup of coffee. She'd just wrapped her robe around herself and she blushed. I was surprised because she had been wearing nothing for the previous hour.

After a pause, while Megan put her hair in a ponytail, she asked if I was going to introduce myself. I did and shook her hand. I told her I was a part-time art student and she told me that she had guessed as much. Then, I described Oak House Deli down the road. It did espresso and served delicious brie and cranberry sandwiches.

Strangely, even though the class had been drawing her curves, wrinkles, and joints, I'd only now noticed the colour of her eyes and the freckles around them.

"You're looking at my freckles, aren't you? I hate this time of year—they always come out."

I told her they were charming freckles. She said she was surprised I hadn't noticed them. From the corner of her eye, she'd seen the 'fierce' look of concentration and permanent frown on my face. I looked at my shoes which were covered in flecks of old red paint.

"Now, I've made *you* blush!" she said, pinching my arm. "Sure, let's have a coffee. You know, you're the first person to even speak to me after one of these things. Most people don't know where to look."

I gathered my leather satchel and held the door for her.

She gestured for me to wait. "You know I have to get dressed first, you lemon. But before we go anywhere you *have* to show me your drawing."

I exaggerated my already shy expression. "Oh no, I mean I'm just starting out; it really isn't very good."

Giving a smirk that paralysed me, she playfully tugged the tube out of my arms, retreating to the desk at the back of the classroom to roll it out.

I stayed by the door as she popped off the lid and placed it down delicately with her thumb and forefinger, as if she were handling a rare artefact. "You know," I said with a dash of panic, "I think Oak House Deli shuts fairly soon. Those sandwiches are really worth it."

I hadn't considered that Megan might want to see my drawing. It was intensely naïve of me. I bolted down the stairs two at a time towards the fire exit, grabbed the pencil from behind my ear, and snapped it in two. Cursing at myself through clenched teeth, I marched across the little courtyard as a few students turned to frown at me.

I couldn't draw well, not elegant human forms anyway. How could I do justice to a beautiful and graceful person like Megan? So, instead I'd stuck to my strengths and looked for those little details that make a person unique.

When I heard a loud knocking on the window behind me, it was Megan in her white robe with my drawing pressed against the glass. She looked angelic, even with a scowl mouthing obscenity-filled interrogatives. She was paler than the high-quality A3 sheet I'd sketched her on.

A funny little birthmark had caught my eye on the milky skin of her neck. It was, no bigger than the palm of a newborn baby's hand. So, I'd focused on that, trying to get it right—its unusual edges like a perforated stamp, the shades that evolved towards the upper part featuring a wiry 12mm long strand of hair surrounded by downy fluff that was so hard to capture with the HB pencil I'd just snapped in two. It had been a challenge to realise on paper but from my position on the other side of the spittle-covered glass two floors below Megan, I could see that on my fourteenth attempt I'd begun to get it right.

I'd attempted each one in a line, so my work resembled a philatelist's dream—an entire sheet of Penny Blacks on display for the campus to see. A few people were looking up at the window too. Megan turned away, my sketch wafting slowly to the classroom floor and out of sight. I might be able to pick it up next Wednesday, but I'd really need to check who was modelling.

# TWANG

I **SWEAR** to God my girlfriend only likes me for my accent. She's a personal trainer, and when I first approached her as she squatted at the gym, she interrupted me to ask where the hell I was from.

I explained, as I often have to, that I was born in Canada but moved to Scotland as a teenager, and spent many subsequent years in South Africa.

"Never heard anyone speak like that, ha!" she said and handed me her card.

Now we live together. I have 24/7 access to her sculpted arse in various stages of undress. But I'm frustrated because she constantly gets me to record messages for her friends, repeating words I pronounce differently like 'mirror', 'fart', and 'muscle'. When I say that last word she always doubles over laughing, then kisses my neck and, if we're somewhere private, she insists we do it there and then.

I'm going to have a word with her though. A serious one. Every time she mimics me, I feel demeaned. I've become more self-conscious when I speak, and my mates say I'm less chatty. I've prepared a little speech, which I'll deliver to her after a deliberate spell of moodiness. I've excluded all the words I know she loves me saying the most. It was tricky because there's a lot of them, but it's important she doesn't fall about laughing and cut me off before I've had a chance to explain.

"Claire," I say, calling to her from the kitchen as I chop up chorizo. "Could you please walk into this room and converse with me about something important."

"Yeah, baby, but why are you talking weird?"

I put the knife down and face her. She recognises my

serious look and I see the edges of her eyes moisten. She nods.

"Listen, I'm aware that you enjoy the sound of my accent. That it provides you with a sense of amusement. I also know it makes you love me in the same way I love your arse. But it's getting me down. I have evolved into a more taciturn person and am self-conscious when speaking with you."

Bizarrely I find myself welling up. She hugs me tightly and I hug her back.

"I'm sorry, baby, I didn't know it bothered you so much. I love the way you speak, that's all."

I feel a little guilty, so I decide to compromise. "Claire, I don't mind now and then. But sometimes it feels like you aren't really listening to me—you're just hearing my accent."

She nods into my shoulder and apologises. She steps back from me and notices that I've left a stain on her top with my fingers.

"Oh, what have you wiped on me here, you little penguin?" she says teasingly.

"Sorry, love, I'm just doing some snacks for us, that's the chorizo, it should wash out."

She bites her bottom lip. "The... what?" she says, pointing at the half cut Spanish sausage on the work surface.

"The *chorizo*, I bought it on the way back from work."

She mumbles something and faces the floor, her eyes pricking with tears as she shakes.

"What is it, Claire?"

"Chorizo!" she roars with laughter, mimicking me, and before I can complain she is planting my face with kisses, and I have my hands all over her perfect arse.

# CONTACT

**A**MELIA stood close to me. My economy-class ticket was getting damp from the tears I'd been wiping from my face. I hugged her again, the red rope marking the queue barrier squished between us. The airport was humid despite the whirring fans. My flight home would be leaving soon, but I didn't want to say goodbye just yet.

Amelia was covering me with kisses and saying something in Spanish. I'd only learnt a few phrases on this trip, but whatever she said was enough to stir the nearby guard.

He turned away to give a little more privacy, she spoke in her heavily accented English. "Even though it short time. I know I love you, Steve."

I was sweating profusely beneath all the layers of local clothing I'd asked Amelia to get for me. As Amelia began to wail, I too broke into a fresh wave of sorrow. Turning awkwardly to the boarding-pass checker and the customs officials beyond, I saw they were all glancing at their watches. My flight was apparently the last that night.

I sobbed into her shoulder and said I really had to go. I squeezed her one more time. "Nos vemos en el sueño esta noche," I shouted walking away, broken.

The immigration officer gave my passport a cursory glance without looking me in the eye. Even one of those ghastly vibrating inhales full of snot and saliva couldn't shift his attention to my face. Me and my touristy goat-leather satchel passed more security guards who shook their heads and muttered as they waved me by. Clearly finding it unusual for a fully grown male to lose the battle against tears. They were embarrassed for me.

At the departure gate, I sat in the corner and gathered myself before the flight closed. Amelia would be back out on the highway now. She was an emotional little thing. I'd depended on that. I thought of our two-day trek in the rainforest near her home. I felt some regrets about the promises I'd made to her since meeting online. The lies I'd let cross my lips as I snuck off into the foliage in the early morning, claiming I was searching for flowers for her. An involuntary squeal caused a ripple of alarm for a few nearby passengers waiting to board. Men frowned at me, but they had no idea of the pain I was in.

This was not a soon-to-be-lonely man emoting the aftermath of a farewell. It was the unique sensation of twelve rare hummingbirds and nine colourful baby finches gently trying to peck their way free of their duct tape home around the edge of my scrotum. New tears had started to run down my face, a worthy distraction.

I hung my headphones around my neck and pressed play so Phil Collins's drums covered the birds' chirps. I swallowed three painkillers. It was going to be a very long but prosperous journey home.

# PRANK

I HID in the cupboard and watched as my four-foot-tall flatmate returned to find his cat was dead. Gavin barely needed to stoop as he petted its rock-hard body, which was now propping open his bedroom door. He burst into tears. I had to bite down on my lip to stifle my sniggers.

I jumped out of the cupboard. "Got you!" I shouted and tossed the cat against the wall. It was a very accurate fake. Gavin dried his eyes, battling a frontier between anger and relief. As his gaze turned upwards and fixed on me his emotions apparently resolved—revenge.

The very next day I discovered that all of my clothes had been dyed pink. In response, I put Gavin's laptop in the oven next to a half-price turkey. They both roasted on gas mark 5 for five hours.

"Gotcha," I yelled when he finally investigated the smell. I woke the next morning with a delicate hangover and discovered half my hair had been shaved off. Gavin stood by my bedside. His tiny hands shook as he giggled.

That night I covered Gavin's new car in superglue and feathers.

In the summer, we took a boys' trip to Indonesia. On arrival, I was pulled out of line at customs and searched. The officials found two kilos of baking flour wrapped in plastic snuck into my suitcase by Gavin. He heaved with laughter as I was cuffed and thrown to the ground. When I was released the next day, Gavin bought me a beer. He'd been laughing ceaselessly, he explained, for over 24 hours.

We went scuba diving the next day. I gestured to Gavin there was an enormous shark behind him. He nearly gave himself the bends as he panicked his way back to the surface.

Rigid with fear over what the other would do next, neither of us expected to sleep easily. After we shared wine on our balcony, however, I soon passed out thanks to the pills Gavin had slipped into my glass.

The tattoo he'd inked on most of my back overnight was a disgraced pop singer who had recently been found in bed with an underage boy. "Gotcha," he said, slapping my back where the skin was still raw.

On our return, I anonymously reported Gavin to the police for hanging around outside a school. I even put up a poster warning parents of Gavin, next to a notice about a dangerous dog. After the ensuing investigation had concluded, he lost his job. "Gotcha," I said. But he didn't smile. His face was on the front of the local paper.

I took a break from pranks for a while. Gavin seemed to have lost his sense of humour. Also, he was late with the rent for the second month, which was so typical of him.

"You can get me back," I told him as he sat homeless on the pavement outside Oak House Deli begging for coins. He answered with a stare, but I knew this was all part of an elaborate ruse.

A few weeks later, when my new flatmate was out, Gavin returned wielding a knife. He lunged at my pelvis, I dodged and we wrestled. Soon blood was pouring from one of us. When I stood up, I saw the blade stuck deeply in Gavin's abdomen. The paramedics said he was dead on arrival. The judge has sentenced me to twenty years for manslaughter.

Sitting in my cell, I watch as my new roomie melts a toothbrush with a contraband lighter. Today I have a visitor. No doubt it'll be Gavin. He probably thinks I'll admit he won. But I still have a few ideas. I'll get him back. The plump little joker. He'll see who the prank's really on and I'll tell him: "Gotcha!"

# KIN

SALLY'S cousin TJ came to stay at my place during the
fashion school summer break. He had long hair that he
swept back over his skull every time he started a new
sentence, and he didn't make eye contact with me as we shook
hands. Despite a decade between them, TJ and Sally got on
well. As I hung my shirts over the bathtub to dry, I heard them
giggling on the sofa.

Sally kissed me hard and said she was grateful for me
putting up with him staying as her place was far too small. In
the same breath she asked me to show TJ a good time and not
to fuss so much.

Despite feeling slightly insulted, I arranged for a table at
a swanky club with a deposit on my credit card. Seeing that
TJ was quietly impressed, I felt quite cool. Although he didn't
condescend to speak or thank me for the champagne. He'd
polished off two glasses before I'd finished a half. Then he
fumbled for something in his back pocket and announced he
was going to the bathroom. I tutted and Sally rubbed my knee
and told me 'Little TJ' was supposed to be on holiday. I topped
up my glass, careful to avoid the icy droplets falling on my
pristine white chinos.

Only a few moments later, I heard girly screams. Standing
up, I saw TJ sporting nothing but his underwear, gyrating
against a pole on the stage. Camera phones flashed as he put
one arm around a scantily clad woman's shoulders, plucked
a bottle of champagne from a Chinese guy's table with the
other, and poured it over her chest.

Sally roared with laughter and applauded TJ's rather
chiselled body along with everybody else. I ran over and

dragged him away.

Outside in the cold street, as Sally helped him do up his shirt buttons, she gave me a look that suggested I'd done something very wrong.

"Let's hit up another club, man!" announced TJ, waving his arms around.

"I think we should head home," I said as sensibly as I could.

"It's barely midnight," she said. "Let's go to Le Jardin like we used to." I winced but she held TJ's hand and marched ahead. Scampering alongside, I told TJ he needed to behave. The people who ran the establishment were not to be trifled with. He burst out laughing and said I needed to 'chillax to the max'.

We found a spot by the bar. TJ immediately started chatting to a sultry woman with a tattoo of a red and black spider on her neck. She fawned over him like someone in a fairy-tale. Sally pinched me and told me to stop staring.

Later, TJ had apparently mustered enough money to purchase me a beverage. He presented me with a shot of tequila. I must admit I felt quite touched—a little guilty even—as I sipped it, and TJ patted my back.

On the dance floor, Sally whispered in my ear, "*Seeing you all laid back like TJ is such a turn-on.*"

Within an hour I was really quite inebriated. Delighted with Sally's renewed attention, I whispered into her ear, "*You know, I remember the big communal bathroom here.*" I winked and led the way. I opened the first cubicle we came to only to find TJ in there holding the tattooed girl up against the wall with his pelvis. She had her finger in his mouth and was smiling.

"Hey, man," said TJ as if we were passing each other in the street.

I shielded Sally's eyes as she giggled. Before I could speak, a bouncer appeared and wrenched my arm behind my back. We were all thrown out.

"Let's go to your place, TJ," said the spider-girl.

I shook my head before TJ could respond.

"It's his holiday!" pleaded Sally handing TJ some cash and my front door key.

Before I could protest, they were on their way to my flat in a grubby taxi. Sally led me into a kebab shop where she fed me chips, played with my hair, and told me I was cool.

My smile was relentless although I couldn't stop thinking about my new bed linen and whether TJ would remember to move my work shirts to the utility room and switch off the hot water tank after they'd showered.

# LISTS

**A**FTER a sudden and upsetting break-up had resulted in misery, absentmindedness, and subsequent unemployment, Anthony decided he needed to get a grip. His new therapist suggested writing lists was an excellent way to maintain control while planning ahead towards a positive future. He'd agreed to give it a shot, and woke early to write his plan for the day: *clean bathroom, get a haircut, replace broken crockery, take out rubbish, mow lawn.* Putting down his pen, he felt elated. His life was really getting back on track.

Beaming, he decided to plan the following day as well: *write CV, go2 job centre, buy potatoes, buy new padlock.* It was as if his old life had vanished and he was living his new life already. Continuing to grin and write, he extended the list: *buy stamps, fix hole in bedroom wall, become an Assistant Manager@ new company, buy car, fire any employees NOT up2 scratch, buy dog, get new flat, go travelling, pick dog up from kennel, write successful novel about travelling, resign from job w/ GOOD bonus, start own fridge magnet company, get married, bury dog & buy new one, have 12 children, go2 France OFTEN, read my novels2 children; wash car, renew passport; retire on good pension, pick Peter up from skool, write memoirs, give Mary & Susan the keys2 my cars, be buried next2 Annabel, leave estate to dog adoption centre.*

He stood up and stretched. His room was covered in Post-it notes and his hand ached. Outside it was dark—too late to get that haircut. "I'll go tomorrow," he thought, smiling at his array of colourful and inspiring ideas. Grabbing a large empty jar from under the sink, he gently removed all the Post-it notes from his fridge door, walls, and dining table and placed each one carefully inside the jar. By the time Anthony had finished, the jar was almost three-quarters full. Opening the back door, he marched confidently towards his shed, clutching the jar to his chest. As he got closer, Annabel's face appeared behind the wire mesh where the glass window of his shed used to be. She began another wave of abuse, full of misunderstandings, threats, and hurtful remarks. He told her to hush, gently reminding her there wasn't a soul around for miles. If she would just hear him out for once—and *really* listen to him this time—she'd be instantly reassured. Sitting on the concrete step, he leaned against the door. Lifting the notes from the jar one by one, he examined each of them like the wings of an exotic butterfly. He read each item earnestly and honestly, smiling at his own thoughtfulness and magnificent potential. Then he posted each note under the tiny gap beneath the door so Annabel could verify his hard work and dedication for herself. Every note punctuated by the monotonous banging of her fists against the walls of the shed.

# DRIFT

THE blizzard strengthened and an entirely new layer of snow settled around us. Visibility was down to a metre. I could only guess where I was on the mountainside, judging it by the incline of the slope where we lay. I held Vicky tightly, trying to share what little body heat I had. With our primitive shelter of branches having blown away, we had to stay awake. Sleep would mean death.

When Vicky's eyes began to droop, I shook her violently and slapped her round the face six times. This was the closest we'd ever been. The rest of our ski party was no doubt drunk around the enormous dining table. Our absence would go unnoticed until the hangovers kicked in tomorrow morning (it was my turn to make breakfast). I'd spent the last few evenings at that table trying to break the ice with Vicky. She was a friend of a friend who I'd met at various things: weddings, birthday dinners, and a New Year's Eve party; she seemed perfect, but I could never get any time alone with her.

The temperature dropped to a futile low, the wind whipping harder, which forced us to shout. "VICKY, I HAVE TO TELL YOU SOMETHING. I HAVE TO TELL YOU SOMETHING… LISTEN. I HAVE TO TELL YOU I REALLY LIKED YOUR HAIR ON SUNDAY MORNING. YOU SHOULD WEAR IT UP MORE OFTEN. IT ENHANCES THE DEPTH AND COMPLEXITY OF YOUR EYES." A snowflake-covered smile appeared on her hazy face. I hugged her tightly and felt relieved to have confessed how I felt.

She responded, at the top of her voice directly in my ear canal, "YOU'RE SO HANDSOME. I LOVE THAT BIG RED JUMPER YOU WEAR. YOU LOOK LIKE AN OLD MAN— SO WARM AND LOVABLE."

She had used the 'L' word, and the strength of that word brought warmth to my heart. It was now imperative that we both survive the night. I also felt a little guilty for leading her away from our party's route. I'd just wanted to be alone with her. I hadn't anticipated we would get lost and caught in a storm.

I decided to announce that I'd developed romantic feelings for her *before* we'd met, based on a photo I'd seen on a friend's fridge door. "IT WAS ONE OF YOU CAMPING WITH DAVE. YOU HAD MUD ON YOUR FACE. I THOUGHT YOU LOOKED FUN."

Although Vicky's face was now practically blue, she *had* told me she *loved* me. I was surprised. I certainly hadn't known about that.

When Vicky started talking about our future, her eyelids dropped but she successfully described the home we'd move into after the wedding. It would have a log fire, old oak beams, and an iron stove in the kitchen. As the relentless cold tightened its grip on us, I rubbed her hands and feet vigorously. She moaned with what I fondly interpreted as a mixture of pleasure and pain, making me promise I'd do this for her every single day when she got home from work. I managed a tooth-chattering grin and she nuzzled into the side of my neck. Feeling moved and losing all inhibitions, I started to sing silly songs to her. I made them up as I went along—puns on her name, jokes about her height and choice of socks—and with each new verse she laughed harder. I continued singing until dawn, until the rays of the rising sun seemed to make the storm vanish.

I carried Vicky down the slope towards our friends' chalet. We weren't that far away after all. As she snoozed in my arms, I glanced down at her ice-encrusted, frozen feet. Most likely, these would be surgically sawn-off stumps by next Tuesday. I knew things wouldn't work out.

# Seams

I THREW my clipboard down and stormed into the toilets to scrub my hands angrily. When I was done, I splashed cold water on my face and watched the droplets roll down my chin in the mirror. A few minutes later Dr Richard King came in and smacked my backside hard. "Not your fault, man. You had made them aware of the risks and you did the best you could." Although I'd automatically expressed similar sentiments to him the previous month when he lost someone on the table, his words still reached me.

Turning to thank Dr King, I saw he was deliberately urinating against the wall and floor by the toilet cubicles. "If you don't smile in the next five seconds, I'll piss on you next," he said, turning his head to face me with a look of menace. I couldn't help but smile. Dr King always could make even the most horrific days bearable. As he swivelled to finally project his stream of piss into the urinal, I looked at the mess he'd made. "Don't worry, old Gregory will clean that up!" he said, doing up his fly. Dr King was referring to the man with clubbed feet who cleaned our department. "He loves the smell of piss!"

I left the toilet, picked up my clipboard, and walked down the corridor to my patient's family. They were huddled together, elbows on knees, waiting for the news. When I tapped the door gently and let myself in, the father stood up like I was royalty. "So, doctor, is Maggie going to be okay?" I asked him to sit, which he did, then I described the complexity of the procedure. This was partly to soften my guilt, but also to delay breaking the unbearable news to them. When I'd finished explaining the challenging nature of the operation,

I looked down, flicking through my papers pointlessly, trying to avoid his gaze. Maggie was dead. Nothing on my clipboard would alter that.

When I turned back to the bereaved father and gave him the news he'd dreaded, the room filled with sobs. I lowered my head solemnly while the family held one another, waves of sheer despair pulsing between them. Staring at my notes, I observed on the final sheet a crude drawing someone had recently scrawled with red pen. It was a man with an enormous smile and cartoonish paperclip legs mopping up a generous pool of steaming liquid. Underneath, in jagged, childish handwriting someone had written '*Gregory's Paradise!*' and signed off '*Dic King*'. Glancing around, I spotted the unmistakable culprit wearing a white coat; he was affecting a hobbling gait along the corridor outside, holding his nose, and smirking.

My lower lip quivered. I bit down hard to take deep breaths through my nostrils. Still, I couldn't help but emit a disquieted squeak, which I attempted to stifle with my free hand. The family looked up as if I'd said something. I stared at the floor, my ribs heaving in agony. The father rushed over, embracing me too and telling me—in a babbling, broken voice—how I'd done everything I could. It was all too much: Dr King's antics in the toilet, the silly drawing, and that poor sod Gregory with his supposed fondness for warm urine. I arched my back and let out an enormous roar of laughter that seemed to make the room shake. No matter what the crisis, Dr King always brought me back from the darkness, ready to fight another day.

# MAN

"**G**RAB *two* extra surface soil samples. O$^2$ levels are fine, over." I grunt and bottle the lifeless dust carefully.

Wintersfield observes me from our outpost a hundred metres away. I see my colleague's deep-socketed stare from his gaunt face through the shimmering light over the dusty surface. The tedium makes each of these expeditions exhausting in a way I can't describe to people at home. I look towards home: a barely perceptible speck in a palette of black oil and stars. My eightieth week on this tiny moon that needed to be checked for potential.

"Come on, Packard, stop messing about," growls Wintersfield into my ear. Both of us irritable to the point of madness, we have nothing left to say. No anecdotes to share. No surprises. No dream pills allowed either, due to the importance of the mission.

We crave other people so much the burden of resentment between us grows constantly. We share only the tiniest of smiles—harder to spot than the Earth—when we cross off another day until our return.

I enter the outpost via the airlock and, as usual, Wintersfield is in the lab chair awaiting the samples. He takes them without a word of thanks. He's won the coin toss three days in a row. The only other time there's a smile, but it only creeps over one of our faces.

I ask if any non-mission-related video messages have arrived, but he doesn't respond. There's the whir of the air purifier and nothing else.

"You know sometimes I see patterns in the dust out there. Reminds me of those crop circles on Earth a few hundred years ago. Did you ever –" I give up, my voice is hollow; I know he won't respond.

As we approach our hundredth week, we begin to chat a little more. Wintersfield mentions the ex-girlfriend again, Katie. He'd like to try again with her. "You never know," he says, "maybe she'll be my nominated co-hab when we find somewhere to colonise."

I nod and think of Cheryl, who is doubtless despairing at how long I've been away, missing me.

Wintersfield tosses the coin. This is the seventeenth day in a row I've lost. We are both superb mathematicians, so the likelihood causes no fascination. He had a run of 19 on his first cycle. Reluctantly, I put on my gear.

Heading out to the patch of rocky caves in sector G4, I consider how despite us drawing a negative on all aspects of potential settlement, Houston XII remains unequivocal. We are to see it through to the full one hundred weeks.

I scrape a sample off an ugly boulder.

"Two from the rocks and one from the ground this time," Wintersfield commands. "Don't bother with that cave, I've done it a hundred times."

His bossiness grates on me. I react by deliberately walking into the cave. I ignore his protests in my earpiece and keep going. After 30 metres, I'm greeted by a brief glow of green light as the walls become fluorescent.

"Are you getting this?" I shout at Wintersfield and point the headcam at the new colours.

I hear him yell for me to turn back, but I ignore him. My eyes are drawn to a green organic mass that, first, slithers up a wall, then, drops in front of me, burrowing itself into the ground in seconds. All it leaves behind is a pool of clear fluid, viscous between my gloved fingers and gone a few moments after.

When I return to the outpost, I find Wintersfield pacing by the time chart instead of his usual place in the lab.

"Did you get all that?" I say. He tosses an open manual at me, marching over and jabbing his finger aggressively at a clause. It clearly states that *any* life forms encountered should be studied without contact pending the arrival of a support craft at the end of another cycle. That would add 18 months to our mission.

"Also, you want to move here with what's-her-name? Cheryl?" he asks.

I say nothing. I watch him as he replaces my samples with others he's apparently kept hidden. My confusion over why he hadn't fixed his broken headcam now gone.

"I'm going to make things up with Katie before Christmas and that's that," he trails off.

In the days leading to our departure, we barely speak. When Houston XII frequently and firmly requests all video data be sent over at once, Wintersfield offers complicated excuses, reiterating that every experiment has resulted in failure; this place could never sustain life. "This lump of coal is completely dry," he spits out over the comms channel before ripping out a few wires. The chief commander's enraged face freezes on the screen in front of us.

Wintersfield heads to his quarters and returns a few moments later clutching a printout of a very pretty woman with blonde hair posing next to a dog. She's wearing wellington boots. So is the dog. Her eyes seem to sparkle. He gently touches her cheek with his finger, then announces he'll start take off procedures soon.

A few minutes later, and I've stuck my tatty image of Cheryl next to his. She is holding a coconut on an artificial beach. I'd paid a small fortune for that coconut at one of the Oak House Bio-Farms. It was our last holiday together before she decided to relocate for a dental hygiene course several hundred miles away. She said she wanted to specialise in perfecting treatments for gingivitis. It was one of the few things the medical community had failed to eradicate. A life-long dream.

Cheryl knew I wouldn't be able to move with her due to my training commitments. She'd packed up everything except the jar that she used to store the cookies she baked me.

Those several hundred miles are nothing but a short step to me now. I see her eyes so full of joy for me, no doubt about it: there are embers that I could stoke for us. Especially since she's seen how much I've done for the planet. Wintersfield gives the photo a nod, seemingly confirming her beauty is sufficient to justify the journey on which we are about to embark, and the rules we are about to break.

Several weeks later, we approach Earth. Even at such distance I can see its dull atmosphere swirls with clouds far browner and more ominous than when we left.

"It's fine," Wintersfield says to me before I can utter a single word of surprise. He slaps a hand on my shoulder and squeezes it in a painful grip. "We need this, mate. A few months checking in with our girls will put us right."

He looks out into the unending darkness that we have come from.

"Besides, I'm pretty sure the other men will be able to find somewhere better. We can rely on them for sure."

# ACKNOWLEDGMENTS

*Sorry Men* is technically a result of my attempts to write creatively since I was teenager desperately in need of orthodontic treatment. With that starting point in mind, there are a number of people to whom I'm grateful for their marvellous influence.

Firstly, I'd like to thank a few of my secondary school teachers. My Theatre Studies teacher, Mrs Clarke. Her enthusiasm, patience, and ability to extract some sense of worth from whatever she observed within the walls of her black-curtained classroom have stayed with me for my whole life. I wouldn't have started writing without her. I'd also like to thank Mr Conquest for reading my adolescent words of fiction over twenty years ago and making me feel like I had some ability, even though what I had shown him was blatantly bloody awful. My A level English Literature teacher Mrs Mumford, for the demonstration of knowledge that was actually required when I was really just mucking about. I wouldn't have got the grade I needed for university without her (or known how to use an apostrophe).

I'm grateful to a number of friends who have been particularly influential in this journey to my first book being published. My dear friend Edward Hadley, for our student radio show work, a decade of nonsensical email exchanges, and allowing me to syphon his enviable wit free of charge since university. Micky McMahon, for the invaluable confidence boosts and encouragement at every single reunion we've had. Ysabelle Cheung, for the opportunity in Hong Kong that got me back into writing and enabled strangers to hear my work. Sam Yates, an inspiring, low-profile genius who can say so much with so few words and render me more productive than ever. Gary Mills for his generosity, energy, and enthusiasm that I could never match. Fliss Trew, for having that slightly disarming skill of always saying exactly what I need to hear.

Since *Sorry Men* started coming together, I was rather spoiled to be given extensive feedback on ropey first drafts. I'd like to thank those people especially. Melissa Saxby (Vant) for her handwritten and insightful comments which she posted halfway across the world. Colette Leung for annotating each story, laughing a lot, and then telling me it wasn't her cup of tea. Kim Haslam, for always reading, commenting, and being absolutely dependable. Nicole Froelich, for her laughter and company at Man Mo Cafe, and being the first person to promote *Sorry Men* before it was even finished by telling diners on tables nearby (who hadn't asked) that I was writing a 'Toilet Book'. Fez Bessant for reading the whole thing bit by bit on his commute, sending an email on each story, then summarising his views over beers in Tsim Sha Tsui one evening. Andrew Daum, one of the cleverest people I know, for always laughing in the right places and his priceless input in the latter stages of editing. Gemma Donald, for not liking it at all because she 'doesn't like twists', but still working through it multiple times because she's a good friend. Ros Howe, for posting me her annotations in her frustratingly perfect handwriting.

Many thanks to those who have read my stories, listened to me, or shared their thoughts on *Sorry Men*. In particular, Matthew Drysdale, Sally Mouse Newton, Oliver Lindon, Sebastian Moreau, Joey Angelakis, Tom Tiding, Christina Colgan, Anthony Hughes, Alejandro Pedro Osorio, Maria Hasnaoui, Johannes Eckold, Meryem Chouirf, Clara Hansen, Laura Hadley, and Vicki Stevenson. I'm also indebted to those who were willing to take the time to write me reviews, Anna Passey, Charlie Schroeder, Ben Tanzer, Doug Stanhope, Jason Tobin, Jason Wong, and Gary Mills.

Finally, et bien sûr, CJ for putting up with it all and so very much more to come.

# PUBLICATION CREDITS

All The Way: *Liars League Hong Kong*, June 2013

The Reunion: *Liars League Hong Kong*, November 2013

All The Signs: *Liars League Hong Kong*, July 2014

The Next Life: *Liars League Hong Kong*, November 2014 & *Hong Kong Spoken Word Festival*, October 2019

All The Reasons: *Liars League Hong Kong*, March 2015

Class: *Liars League Hong Kong*, June 2015

Catch: *Liars League Hong Kong*, February 2018

Mo Exit: *Liars League Hong Kong*, December 2019

Prank: *Mono.*, July 17th 2021

Accumulator: *Reflex Press*, August 21st 2021

Tales: *Mono.* August 26th 2021

Carriage: *Litro.* November 19th 2021

Man: *Fragmented Voices*, 'Heart/h' Anthology, 21st November 2021

Rummage: *Litro.* 30th June 2023

Break: *Coffin Bell*, Volume 6 Issue 3, 2nd July 2023